"Got a problem?"

C.C. asked. She was well aware that his gaze had drifted down to the neck of her overalls. She was used to that. But she didn't have to like it.

"You're the mechanic?"

"No, I'm the interior decorator."

Trent glanced around the garage, with its oil-splattered floor and cluttered work tables. "You do very interesting work." He paused. "If you're free tonight, maybe you could help me sample some of the local seafood. We could discuss my carburetor."

Flustered and flattered, C.C. reached out to accept the credit card he offered. Then she saw the name imprinted there—Trenton St. James III.

It figured, she thought. Fancy car, fancy suit, fancy manners. She should have spotted it right off. "Sign here." Trent signed, and she tossed his keys to him. Or rather *at* him. He snagged them just before they hit his face.

"A simple no would have done the job."

"Men like you don't understand a simple no. If I'd known who you were, I'd have drilled holes in your muffler."

Dear Reader,

June is traditionally the month of weddings, and at Silhouette Romance, wedding bells are definitely ringing! Our heroines this month will fulfill their hearts' desires with the kinds of heroes you've always dreamed of—from the dark, mysterious stranger to the lovable boy-next-door. Silhouette Romance novels *always* reflect the magic of love—sweeping you away with heartwarming, poignant stories that will move you time and time again.

In the next few months, we'll be publishing romances by many of your all-time favorites, including Diana Palmer, Brittany Young and Annette Broadrick. And, as promised, Nora Roberts begins her CALHOUN WOMEN series this month with the Silhouette Romance, *Courting Catherine*.

WRITTEN IN THE STARS is a very special event for 1991. Each month, we're proud to present a Silhouette Romance that focuses on the hero—and his astrological sign. June features one of the most enigmatic, challenging men of all—*The Gemini Man*. Our authors and editors have created this delightfully romantic series especially for you, the reader, and we'd love to hear what you think. After all, at Silhouette Romance, we take our readers' comments to heart!

Please write to us at Silhouette Romance
                     300 East 42nd Street
                     New York, NY 10017

We look forward to hearing from you!

Sincerely,

Valerie Susan Hayward
Senior Editor

NORA ROBERTS

Courting Catherine

Silhouette *Romance*
Published by Silhouette Books New York
America's Publisher of Contemporary Romance

To Maxine,
For being my friend as well as my sister

SILHOUETTE BOOKS
300 E. 42nd St., New York, N.Y. 10017

COURTING CATHERINE

ISBN: 0-373-08801-9

First Silhouette Books printing June 1991

Printed in the U.S.A.

Books by Nora Roberts

Silhouette Romance

Irish Thoroughbred #81
Blithe Images #127
Song of the West #143
Search for Love #163
Island of Flowers #180
From This Day #199
Her Mother's Keeper #215
Untamed #252
Storm Warning #274
Sullivan's Woman #280
Less of a Stranger #299
Temptation #529
‡*Courting Catherine* #801

Silhouette Special Edition

The Heart's Victory #59
Reflections #100
Dance of Dreams #116
First Impressions #162
The Law Is a Lady #175
Opposites Attract #199
*Playing the Odds #225
*Tempting Fate #235
**All the Possibilities* #247
**One Man's Art* #259
Summer Desserts #271
Second Nature #288
One Summer #306
Lessons Learned #318
A Will and a Way #345
**For Now, Forever* #361
Local Hero #427
°*The Last Honest Woman* #451
°*Dance to the Piper* #463
°*Skin Deep* #475
Loving Jack #499
Best Laid Plans #511
The Welcoming #553
Taming Natasha #583
°*Without a Trace* #625

Silhouette Intimate Moments

Once More with Feeling #2
Tonight and Always #12
This Magic Moment #25
Endings and Beginnings #33
A Matter of Choice #49
Rules of the Game #70
The Right Path #85
Partners #94
Boundary Lines #114
Dual Image #123
The Art of Deception #131
†*Affaire Royale* #142
Treasures Lost, Treasures Found #150
Risky Business #160
Mind Over Matter #185
†*Command Performance* #198
†*The Playboy Prince* #212
Irish Rose #232
The Name of the Game #264
Gabriel's Angel #300
Time Was #313
Times Change #317
Night Shift #365
Night Shadow #373

Silhouette Books

Silhouette Christmas Stories 1986
"Home for Christmas"
Silhouette Summer Sizzlers 1989
"Impulse"

‡The Calhoun Women

*MacGregor Series

°The O'Hurleys!

†Cordina's Royal Family

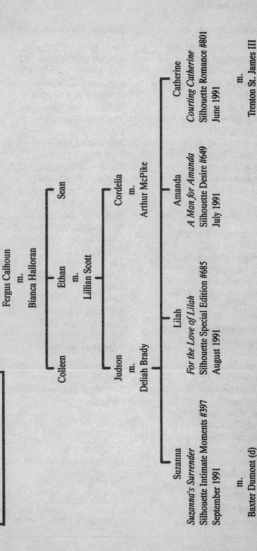

THE CALHOUN WOMEN

Fergus Calhoun
m.
Bianca Halloran

Colleen   Ethan   Sean
                  m.
              Lillian Scott

Judson   Cordelia
m.   m.
Deliah Brady   Arthur McPike

Suzanna   Lilah   Amanda   Catherine

Suzanna's Surrender   *For the Love of Lilah*   *A Man for Amanda*   *Courting Catherine*
Silhouette Intimate Moments #397   Silhouette Special Edition #685   Silhouette Desire #649   Silhouette Romance #801
September 1991   August 1991   July 1991   June 1991

m.   m.
Baxter Dumont (d)   Trenton St. James III

Alex   Jenny

Prologue

Bar Harbor, Maine
June 12, 1912

I saw him on the cliffs overlooking Frenchman Bay. He was tall and dark and young. Even from a distance, as I walked with little Ethan's hand in mine, I could see the defiant set of his shoulders. He held the brush as though it were a saber, his palette like a shield. Indeed it seemed to me that he was dueling with his canvas rather than painting on it. So deep was his concentration, so fast and fierce the flicks of his wrist, one would have thought his life depended on what he created there.

Perhaps it did.

I thought it odd, even amusing. My image of artists had always been one of gentle souls who see things we mortals cannot, and suffer in their quest to create them for us.

Yet I knew, before he turned and looked at me, that I would not see a gentle face.

It seemed that he was the product of an artist himself. A rough sculptor who had shorn away at an oak slab, carving out a high brow, dark hooded eyes, a long straight nose and full sensual mouth. Even the sweep of his hair might have been hewn from some ebony wood.

How he stared at me! Even now I can feel the heat rise to my face and the dampness spring to my palms. The wind was in his hair, sweet and moist from the sea, and ruffled the loose shirt he wore that was splattered and streaked from his paint. With the rocks and sky at his back, he looked very proud, very angry, as if he owned this jut of land—or the entire island—and I was the intruder.

He stood in silence for what seemed like forever, his eyes so intense, so fierce somehow that my tongue cleaved to the roof of my mouth. Then little Ethan began to babble and tug at my hand. The angry glare in his eyes softened. He smiled. I know a heart does not stop at such moments. And yet . . .

I found myself stammering, apologizing for the intrusion, lifting Ethan into my arms before my bright and curious little boy could rush forward toward the rocks.

He said, "Wait."

And taking up pad and pencil began to sketch as I stood immobile and trembling for reasons I cannot fathom. Ethan stilled and smiled, somehow as mesmerized by the man as I. I could feel the sun on my back and the wind on my face, could smell the water and the wild roses.

"Your hair should be loose," he said, and, putting the pencil aside, walked toward me. *"I've painted sunsets that were less dramatic."* He reached out and touched Ethan's bright red hair. *"You share the color with your young brother."*

"My son." Why was my voice so breathless? *"He is my son. I'm Mrs. Fergus Calhoun,"* I said while his eyes seemed to devour my face.

"Ah, The Towers." He looked beyond me then to where the peaks and turrets of our summer home could be seen on the higher cliff above. *"I've admired your house, Mrs. Calhoun."*

Before I could reply, Ethan was reaching out, laughing, and the man scooped him up. I could only stare as he stood with his back to the wind, holding my child, jiggling him easily on his hip.

"A fine boy."

"And an energetic one. I thought to take him for a walk to give his nanny a bit of a rest. She has less trouble with my two other children combined than with young Ethan."

"You have other children?"

"Yes, a girl, a year older than Ethan, and a baby, not quite one. We only arrived for the season yesterday. Do you live on the island?"

"For now. Will you pose for me, Mrs. Calhoun?"

I blushed. But beneath the embarrassment was a deep and dreamy pleasure. Still, I knew the impropriety and Fergus's temper. So I refused, politely, I hoped. He did not persist, and I am ashamed to say that I felt a keen disappointment. When he gave Ethan back to me, his eyes were on mine—a deep slate gray that seemed to see more than my face. Perhaps more *than anyone had seen before. He bid me good day, so I turned to walk with my child back to The Towers, my home and my duties.*

I knew as surely as if I had turned to look, that he watched me until I was hidden by the cliff. My heart thundered.

Chapter One

Bar Harbor
1991

Trenton St. James III was in a foul mood. He was the kind of man who expected doors to open when he knocked, phones to be answered when he dialed. What he did not expect, and hated to tolerate, was having his car break down on a narrow two-lane road ten miles from his destination. At least the car phone had allowed him to track down the closest mechanic. He hadn't been overly thrilled about riding into Bar Harbor in the cab of the tow truck while strident rock had bellowed from the speakers and his rescuer had sung along, off-key, in between bites of an enormous ham sandwich.

"Hank, you just call me Hank, ayah," the driver had told him then took a long pull from a bottle of soda. "C.C.'ll fix you up all right and tight. Best damn mechanic in Maine, you ask anybody."

Trent decided, under the circumstances, he'd have to take just-call-me-Hank's word for it. To save time and trouble, he'd had the driver drop him off in the village with directions to the garage and a grimy business card Trent studied while holding it gingerly at the corners.

But as with any situation Trent found himself in, he decided to make it work for him. While his car was being dealt with, he made half a dozen calls to his office back in Boston—putting the fear of God into a flurry of secretaries, assistants and junior vice-presidents. It put him in a slightly better frame of mind.

He lunched on the terrace of a small restaurant, paying more attention to the paperwork he took from his briefcase than the excellent lobster salad or balmy spring breeze. He checked his watch often, drank too much coffee and, with impatient brown eyes, studied the traffic that streamed up and down the street.

Two of the waitresses on lunch shift discussed him at some length. It was early April, several weeks before the height of the season, so the restaurant wasn't exactly hopping with customers.

They agreed that this one was a beaut, from the top of his dark blond head to the tips of his highly polished Italian shoes. They agreed that he was a businessman, and an *important* one, because of the leather briefcase and spiffy gray suit and tie. Plus, he wore cuff links. Gold ones.

They decided, as they rolled flatware into napkins for the next shift, that he was young for it, no more than thirty. Outrageously handsome was their unanimous vote while they took turns refilling his coffee cup and getting closer looks. Nice clean features, they agreed, with a kind of polished air that would have been just a tad slick if it hadn't been for the eyes.

They were dark and broody and impatient, making the waitresses speculate as to whether he'd been stood up by a woman. Though they couldn't imagine any female in her right mind doing so.

Trent paid no more attention to them than he would have to anyone who performed a paid service. That disappointed them. The whopping tip he left made up for it nicely. It would have surprised him that the tip would have meant more to the waitresses if he had offered a smile with it.

He relocked his briefcase and prepared to take the brisk walk to the mechanic at the end of town. He wasn't a cold man and wouldn't have considered himself aloof. As a St. James he had grown up with servants who had quietly and efficiently gone about the business of making his life simpler. He paid well, even generously. If he didn't show any overt appreciation or personal interest, it was simply because it never occurred to him.

At the moment, his mind was on the deal he hoped to close by the end of the week. Hotels were his business, with the emphasis on luxury and resorts. The summer before, Trent's father had located a particular property while he and his fourth wife had been yachting in Frenchman Bay. While Trenton St. James II's instincts as to women were notoriously skewed, his business instincts were always on target.

He'd begun negotiations almost immediately for the buy of the enormous stone house overlooking Frenchman Bay. His appetite had been whetted by the reluctance of the owners to sell what had to be a white elephant as a private home. As expected, the senior Trenton had been turning things his way, and the deal was on the way to being set.

Then Trent had found the whole business dumped into his lap as his father was once again tangled in a complicated divorce.

Wife number four had lasted almost eighteen months, Trent mused. Which was two months longer than wife number three. Trent accepted, fatalistically, that there was bound to be a number five around the corner. The old man was as addicted to marriage as he was to real estate.

Trent was determined to close the deal on The Towers before the ink had dried on this last divorce decree. As soon as he got his car out of the garage, he would drive up and take a firsthand look at the place.

Because of the time of year, many of the shops were closed as he walked through town, but he could see the possibilities. He knew that during the season the streets of Bar Harbor were crammed with tourists with credit cards and travelers' checks at the ready. And tourists needed hotels. He had the statistics in his briefcase. With solid planning, he figured The Towers would cull a hefty percentage of that tourist trade within fifteen months.

All he had to do was convince four sentimental women and their aunt to take the money and run.

He checked his watch again as he turned the corner toward the mechanic's. Trent had given him precisely two hours to deal with whatever malfunction the BMW had suffered. That, he was convinced, was enough.

Of course he could have taken the company plane up from Boston. It would have been more practical, and Trent was nothing if not a practical man. But he'd wanted to drive. Needed to, he admitted. He'd needed those few hours of quiet and solitude.

Business was booming, but his personal life was going to hell.

Who would have thought that Marla would suddenly shove an ultimatum down his throat? Marriage or nothing. It still baffled him. She had known since the beginning of their relationship that marriage had never been an option. He had no intention of taking a ride on the roller coaster his father seemed to thrive on.

Not that he wasn't—hadn't been—fond of her. She was lovely and well-bred, intelligent and successful in her field of fashion design. With Marla, there was never a hair out of place, and Trent appreciated that kind of meticulousness in a woman. Just as he had appreciated her practical attitude toward their relationship.

She had claimed not to want marriage or children or pledges of undying love. Trent considered it a personal betrayal that she suddenly changed her tune and demanded it all.

He hadn't been able to give it to her.

They had parted, stiff as strangers, only two weeks before. She was already engaged to a golf pro.

It stung. But even as it stung, it convinced him he had been right all along. Women were unstable, fickle creatures, and marriage was a bloodless kind of suicide.

She hadn't even loved him. Thank God. She had simply wanted "commitment and stability," as she had put it. Trent felt, smugly, that she would soon find out marriage was the last place to find either.

Because he knew it was unproductive to dwell on mistakes, he allowed thoughts of Marla to pass out of his mind. He would take a vacation from females, he decided.

Trent paused outside the white cinder-block building with its scatter of cars in the lot. The sign over the open garage doors read C.C.'s Automovation. Just beneath the title, which Trent found ostentatious, was an offer of twenty-four-hour towing, complete auto repairs and refinishing—foreign and domestic—and free estimates.

Through the doors, he could hear rock music. Trent let out a sigh as he went in.

The hood was up on his BMW, and a pair of dirty boots peeked out from beneath the car. The mechanic was tapping the toes of the boots together in time to the din of music. Frowning, Trent glanced around the garage area. It smelled of grease and honeysuckle—a ridiculous combination. The place itself was a disorganized and grimy mess of tools and auto parts, something that looked as though it might have been a fender, and a coffee maker that was boiling whatever was inside it down to black sludge.

There was a sign on the wall that stated No Checks Cashed, Not Even For You.

Several others listed services provided by the shop and their rates. Trent supposed they were reasonable, but he had no yardstick. There were two vending machines against a wall, one offering soft drinks, the other junk food. A coffee can held change that customers were free to contribute to or take from. An interesting concept, Trent thought.

"Excuse me," he said. The boots kept right on tapping. "Excuse me," he repeated, louder. The music upped its tempo and so did the boots. Trent nudged one with his shoe.

"What?" The answer from under the car was muffled and annoyed.

"I'd like to ask you about my car."

"Get in line." There was the clatter of a tool and a muttered curse.

Trent's eyebrows lifted then drew together in a manner that made his subordinates quake. "Apparently I'm the first in line already."

"Right now you're behind this idiot's oil pan. Save me from rich yuppies who buy a car like this then don't bother to find out the difference between a carburetor and a tire iron. Hold on a minute, buddy, or talk to Hank. He's around somewhere."

Trent was still several sentences back at "idiot." "Where's the proprietor?"

"Busy. Hank!" The mechanic's voice lifted to a roar. "Damn it. Hank! Where the devil did he take off to?"

"I couldn't say." Trent marched over to the radio and flicked off the music. "Would it be too much to ask you to come out from under there and tell me the status of my car?"

"Yeah." From the vantage point under the BMW, C.C. studied the Italian loafers and took an immediate dislike to them. "I got my hands full at the moment. You can come down here and lend one of yours if you're in such a hurry, or drive over to McDermit's in Northeast Harbor.''

"I can hardly drive when you're under my car.'' Though the idea held a certain appeal.

"This yours?'' C.C. sniffed and tightened bolts. The guy had a fancy Boston accent to go with the fancy shoes. "When's the last time you had this thing tuned? Changed the points and plugs, the oil?''

"I don't—''

"I'm sure you don't.'' There was a clipped satisfaction in the husky voice that had Trent's jaw tightening. "You know, you don't just buy a car, but a responsibility. A lot of people don't pull down an annual salary as rich as the sticker price on a machine like this. With reasonable care and maintenance, this baby would run for your grandchildren. Cars aren't disposable commodities, you know. People make them that way because they're too lazy or too stupid to take care of the basics. You needed a lube job six months ago.''

Trent's fingers drummed on the side of his briefcase. "Young man, you're being paid to service my car, not to lecture me on my responsibilities to it.'' In a habit as ingrained as breathing, he checked his watch. "Now, I'd like to know when my car will be ready, as I have a number of appointments.''

"Lecture's free.'' C.C. gave a push and sent the creeper scooting out from under the car. "And I'm not your young man.''

That much was quite obvious. Though the face was grimy and the dark hair cropped boyishly short, the body clad in greasy coveralls was decidely feminine. Every curvy inch of it. Trent wasn't often thrown for a loss, but now he simply stood, staring as C.C. rose from the creeper and faced him, tapping a wrench against her palm.

Looking beyond the smears of black on her face, Trent could see she had very white skin in contrast with her ebony hair. Beneath the fringe of bangs, her forest-green eyes were narrowed. Her full, unpainted lips were pursed in what, under different circumstances, would have been a very sexy pout. She was tall for a woman and built like a goddess. It was she, Trent realized, who smelled of motor oil and honeysuckle.

"Got a problem?" she asked him. C.C. was well aware that his gaze had drifted down from the neck of her coveralls to the cuffs and back again. She was used to it. But she didn't have to like it.

The voice had an entirely different effect when a man realized those dark, husky tones belonged to a woman. "You're the mechanic!"

"No, I'm the interior decorator."

Trent glanced around the garage with its oil-splattered floor and cluttered worktables. He couldn't resist. "You do very interesting work."

Letting the breath out between her teeth, she tossed the wrench onto a workbench. "Your oil and air filter needed to be changed. The timing was off and the carburetor needed some adjusting. You still need a lube job and your radiator should be flushed."

"Will it run?"

"Yeah, it'll run." C.C. took a rag out of her pocket and began to wipe her hands. She judged him as the kind of man who took better care of his ties than he did of his car. With a shrug, she stuck the rag back into her pocket. It was no concern of hers. "Come through to the office and we can settle up."

She led the way through the door at the rear of the garage, into a narrow hallway that angled into a glass-walled office. It was cramped with a cluttered desk, thick parts catalogues, a half-full gum ball machine and two wide swivel chairs. C.C. sat and, in the un-canny way of people who heap papers on their desk, put her hand unerringly on her invoices.

"Cash or charge?" she asked him.

"Charge." Absently he pulled out his wallet. He wasn't sexist. Trent assured himself he was not. He had meticulously made certain that women were given the same pay and opportunity for promotion in his company as any male on his staff. It never occurred to him to be concerned whether employees were males or females, as long as they were efficient, loyal and de-pendable. But the longer he looked at the woman who sat busily filling out the invoice, the more he was cer-tain she didn't fit his or anyone's image of an auto mechanic.

"How long have you worked here?" It surprised him to hear himself ask. Personal questions weren't his style.

"On and off since I was twelve." Those dark green eyes flicked up to his. "Don't worry. I know what I'm doing. Any work that's done in my shop is guaran-teed."

"Your shop?"

"My shop."

She unearthed a calculator and began to figure the total with long, elegantly shaped fingers that were still grimy.

He was putting her back up. Maybe it was the shoes, she thought. Or the tie. There was something arrogant about a maroon tie. "That's the damage." C.C. turned the invoice around and started down the list point by point.

He wasn't paying any attention, which was totally out of character. This was a man who read every word of every paper that crossed his desk. But he was looking at her, frankly fascinated.

"Any questions?" She glanced up and found her gaze locked with his. She could almost hear the click.

"You're C.C.?"

"That's right." She was forced to clear her throat. Ridiculous, she told herself. He had ordinary eyes. Maybe a little darker, a bit more intense than she had noted at first, but still ordinary. There was no earthly reason why she couldn't look away from them. But she continued to stare. If she had been of a fanciful state of mind—which she assured herself she was not—she would have said the air thickened.

"You have grease on your cheek," he said quietly, and smiled at her.

The change was astonishing. He went from being an aloof, annoying man to a warm and approachable one. His mouth softened as it curved, the impatience in his eyes vanished. There was humor there now, an easy, inviting humor that was irresistible. C.C. found herself smiling back.

"It goes with the territory." Maybe she'd been a tad abrupt, she thought, and made an effort to correct it. "You're from Boston, right?"

"Yes. How did you know?"

Her lips remained curved as she shrugged. "Between the Massachusetts plates and your speech pattern, it wasn't hard. We get a lot of trade from Boston on the island. Are you here on vacation?"

"Business." Trent tried to remember the last time he'd taken a vacation, and couldn't quite pin it down. Two years? he wondered. Three?

C.C. pulled a clipboard from under a pile of catalogues and scanned the next day's schedule. "If you're going to be around for a while, we could fit that lube job in tomorrow."

"I'll keep it in mind. You live on the island?"

"Yes. All my life." The chair creaked as she brought her long legs up to sit Indian-style. "Have you been to Bar Harbor before?"

"When I was a boy, I spent a couple of weekends here with my mother." Lifetimes ago, he thought. "Maybe you could recommend some restaurants or points of interest. I might squeeze in some free time."

"You shouldn't miss the park." After unearthing a sheet of memo paper, she began to write. "You really can't go wrong anywhere as far as seafood, and it's early enough in the season that you shouldn't have any problem with crowds and lines." She offered the paper, which he folded and slipped into his breast pocket.

"Thanks. If you're free tonight maybe you could help me sample some of the local seafood. We could discuss my carburetor."

Flustered and flattered, she reached out to accept the credit card he offered. She was on the point of agreeing when she read the name imprinted there. "Trenton St. James III."

"Trent," he said easily, and smiled again.

It figured, C.C. thought. Oh, it absolutely figured. Fancy car, fancy suit, fancy manners. She should have spotted it right off. She should have *smelled* it. Seething, she imprinted the card on the credit card form. "Sign here."

Trent took out a slim gold pen and signed while she rose and stalked over to a pegboard to retrieve his keys. He glanced over just as she tossed them to him. *At* him was more accurate. He managed to snag them before they hit his face. He jingled them lightly in his hand as she stood, hands on hips, face dark with fury.

"A simple no would have done the job."

"Men like you don't understand a simple no." C.C. turned to the glass wall, then whirled back. "If I'd known who you were, I'd have drilled holes in your muffler."

Slowly Trent slipped the keys into his pocket. His temper was renowned. It wasn't hot—that would have been easier to dodge. It was ice. As he stood it slid through him, frosting his eyes, tightening his mouth, coating his voice. "Would you like to explain?"

She strode toward him until they were toe to toe and eye to eye. "I'm Catherine Colleen Calhoun. And I want you to keep your greedy hands off my house."

Trent said nothing for a moment as he adjusted his thoughts. Catherine Calhoun, one of the four sisters who owned The Towers—and one who apparently had strong feelings regarding the sale. Since he was going to have to maneuver around all four of them, he might as well start here. And now.

"A pleasure, Miss Calhoun."

"Not mine." She reached down and ripped off his copy of the credit card receipt. "Get your butt back in your big, bad BMW and head back to Boston."

"A fascinating alliteration." Still watching her, Trent folded the paper and put it into his pocket. "You, however, are not the only party involved."

"You're not going to turn my house into one of your glossy hotels for bored debutantes and phony Italian counts."

He nearly smiled at that. "You've stayed in one of the St. James hotels?"

"I don't have to, I know what they're like. Marble lobbies, glass elevators, twenty-foot chandeliers and fountains spurting everywhere."

"You have something against fountains?"

"I don't want one in my living room. Why don't you go foreclose on some widows and orphans and leave us alone?"

"Unfortunately, I don't have any foreclosures scheduled this week." He held up a hand when she snarled. "Miss Calhoun, I've come here at the request of your liaison. Whatever your personal feelings, there are three other owners of The Towers. I don't intend to leave until I've spoken with them."

"You can talk until your lungs collapse, but...what liaison?"

"Mrs. Cordelia Calhoun McPike."

C.C.'s color fluctuated a bit, but she didn't back down. "I don't believe you."

Without a word, Trent set his briefcase down onto the piles of paper on her desk and flipped the combination. From one of his neatly ordered files he withdrew a letter written on heavy ivory paper. C.C.'s heart dropped a little. She snatched it from him and read.

Dear Mr. St. James,
The Calhoun women have taken your offer to The Towers under consideration. As this is a complex situation, we feel it would be in everyone's best interest to discuss the terms in person, rather than communicating by letter.

As their representative, I would like to invite you to The Towers—*(C.C. gave a strangled groan)*—for a few days. I believe this more personal approach will be of mutual benefit. I'm sure you'll agree that having a closer, more informal look at the property that interests you will be an advantage.

Please feel free to contact me, at The Towers, if you are amenable to the arrangement.

Very truly yours,
Cordelia Calhoun McPike

C.C. read it through twice, grinding her teeth. She would have crumpled the letter into a ball if Trent hadn't rescued it and slipped it back into its file.

"I take it you weren't apprised of the arrangement?"

"Apprised? Damn straight I wasn't apprised. That meddlesome old... Oh, Aunt Coco, I'm going to murder you."

"I assume Mrs. McPike and Aunt Coco are one and the same person."

"Some days it's hard to tell." She turned back. "But either way, both of them are dead."

"I'll sidestep the family violence, if you don't mind."

C.C. stuck her hands into her coverall pockets and glared at him. "If you still intend to stay at The Towers, you're going to be neck deep in it."

He nodded, accepting. "Then I'll take my chances."

Chapter Two

Aunt Coco was busily arranging hothouse roses in two of the Dresden vases that had yet to be sold. She hummed a current rock hit as she worked, occasionally adding a quick bum-bum-bum or ta-te-da. Like the other Calhoun women, she was tall, and liked to think that her figure, which had thickened only a little in the past decade, was regal.

She had dressed and groomed carefully for the occasion. Her short, fluffy hair was tinted red this week and pleased her enormously. Vanity was not a sin or character flaw in Coco's estimation, but a woman's sacred duty. Her face, which was holding up nicely, thank you, from the lift she'd had six years before, was scrupulously made up. Her best pearls swung at her ears and encircled her neck. Coco decided, with a quick glance in the hall mirror, that the black jumpsuit was both dramatic and sleek. The backless heels she wore slapped satisfactorily against the chestnut floor and had her teetering at six foot.

An imposing and, yes, regal figure, she bustled from room to room, checking and rechecking every detail. Her girls might be just a tiny bit upset with her for inviting company without mentioning it. But she could always claim absentmindedness. Which she did whenever it suited her.

Coco was the younger sister of Judson Calhoun, who had married Deliah Brady and sired four girls. Judson and Deliah, whom Coco had loved dearly, had been killed fifteen years before when their private plane had gone down over the Atlantic.

Since then, she had done her best to be father and mother and friend to her beautiful little orphans. A widow for nearly twenty years, Coco was a striking woman with a devious mind and a heart the consistency of marshmallow cream. She wanted, was determined to have, the best for her girls. Whether they liked it or not. With Trenton St. James's interest in The Towers, she saw an opportunity.

She didn't care a bit whether he bought the rambling fortress of a house. Though God knows how much longer they could hold on to it in any case, what with taxes and repairs and heating bills. As far as she was concerned, Trenton St. James III could take it or leave it. But she had a plan.

Whether he took or left it, he was going to fall head over bank account with one of the girls. She didn't know which one. She'd tried her crystal ball but hadn't come up with a name.

But she knew. She had known the moment the first letter had come. The boy was going to sweep one of her darlings away into a life of love and luxury.

She'd be damned if any one of them would have one without the other.

With a sigh, she adjusted the taper in its Lalique holder. She had been able to give them love, but the luxury... If Judson and Deliah had lived, things would have been different. Surely Judson would have pulled himself out of the financial difficulty he'd been suffering. With his cleverness, and Deliah's drive, it would have been a very temporary thing.

But they hadn't lived, and money had become an increasing problem. How she hated to have to sell off the girls' inheritance piece by piece just to keep the sagging roof they all loved over their heads.

Trenton St. James III was going to change all that by falling madly in love with one of her darling babies.

Maybe it would be Suzanna, she thought, plumping the pillows on the parlor sofa. Poor little dear with her heart broken by the worthless cur she had married. Coco's lips tightened. To think he had fooled all of them. Even her! He had made her baby's life a misery, then had divorced her to marry that busty bimbo.

Coco let out a disgusted breath then cast a beady eye on the cracked plaster in the ceiling. She would have to make sure that Trenton would suit as a father to Suzanna's two children. And if he didn't . . .

There was Lilah, her own lovely free spirit. Her Lilah needed someone who would appreciate her lively mind and eccentric ways. Someone who would nurture and settle. Just a bit. Coco wouldn't tolerate anyone who would try to smother her darling girl's mystical bent.

Perhaps it would be Amanda. Coco twitched a drapery so that it covered a mouse hole. Hardheaded, practical-minded Amanda. Now that would be a match! The successful businessman and woman, wheeling and dealing. But he would have to have a softer side, one that recognized that Mandy needed to be cherished, as well as respected. Even if she didn't recognize it herself.

With a satisfied sigh, Coco moved from parlor to sitting room, from sitting room to library, library to study.

Then there was C.C. Shaking her head, Coco adjusted a picture so that it hid—almost—the watermarks on the aging silk wallpaper. That child had inherited the Calhoun stubbornness in spades. Imagine, a lovely girl wasting her life diddling with engines and fuel pumps. A grease monkey. Lord save us.

It was doubtful that a man like Trenton St. James III would be interested in a woman who spent all of her time under a car. Then again, C.C. was the baby of the family at twenty-three. Coco felt that she had more than enough time to find her little girl the perfect husband.

The stage was set, she decided. And soon, Mr. St. James would be walking into Act One.

The front door slammed. Coco winced, knowing that the vibration would have pictures jittering on the walls and crockery dancing on tables. She worked her way through the winding maze of rooms, tidying as she went.

"Aunt Coco!"

Coco's hand lifted automatically to pat her breast. She recognized C.C.'s voice, and the fury in it. Now what could have happened to fire the girl up? she wondered, and put on her best sympathetic smile.

"Just coming, dear. I didn't expect you home for hours yet. It's such a pleasant…" She trailed off as she saw her niece, stripped down to fighting weight in torn jeans and a T-shirt, traces of grease still on her face and the hands she had fisted and jammed at her hips. And the man behind her—the man Coco recognized as her prospective nephew-in-law. "Surprise," she finished, and pasted the smile back into place. "Why, Mr. St. James, how lovely." She stepped forward, hand extended. "I'm Mrs. McPike."

"How do you do?"

"It's so nice to meet you at last. I hope you had a pleasant trip."

"An…interesting one, all in all."

"Even better than pleasant." She patted his hand before releasing it, approving his level gaze and well-pitched voice. "Please, come in. I believe a person should begin as they mean to go on, so I want you to begin to make yourself at home right now. I'll just fix us all some tea."

"Aunt Coco," C.C. said in a low voice.

"Yes, dear, would you like something other than tea?"

"I want an explanation, and I want it now."

Coco's heart hammered a bit, but she gave her niece an open, slightly curious smile. "Explanation? For what?"

"I want to know what the hell he's doing here."

"Catherine, really!" Coco tsk-tsked. "Your manners, one of my very few failures. Come, Mr. St. James—or may I call you Trenton—you must be a bit frazzled after the drive. You did say you were driving? Why don't we just go in and sit in the parlor?" She was easing him along as she spoke. "Marvelous weather for a drive, isn't it?"

"Hold it." C.C. moved quickly and planted herself in their path. "Hold it. Hold it. You're not tucking him up in the parlor with tea and small talk. I want to know why you invited him here."

"C.C." Coco gave a long-suffering sigh. "Business is more pleasant and more successful on all sides when it's conducted in person, and in a relaxed atmosphere. Wouldn't you agree, Trenton?"

"Yes." He was surprised that he had to hold back a grin. "Yes, I would."

"There."

"Not another step." C.C. flung out both hands. "We haven't agreed to sell."

"Of course not," Coco said patiently. "That's why Trenton is here. So we can discuss all the options and possibilities. You really should go up and wash before tea, C.C. You've engine grease or whatever on your face."

With the heel of her hand, C.C. rubbed at it. "Why wasn't I told he was coming?"

Coco blinked and tried to leave her eyes slightly unfocused. "Told? Why, of course, you were told. I would hardly have invited company without telling all of you."

Face mutinous, C.C. held her ground. "You didn't tell me."

"Now, C.C., I..." Coco pursed her lips, knowing—since she'd practiced in the mirror—that it made her look befuddled. "I didn't? Are you certain? I would have sworn I told you and the girls the minute I got Mr. St. James's acceptance."

"No," C.C. said flatly.

"Oh, my." Coco lifted her hands to her cheeks. "Oh, how awful, really. I must apologize. What a dreadful mix-up. And all my fault. C.C., I do beg your pardon. After all, this is your house, yours and your sisters'. I would never presume on your good nature and your hospitality by..."

Before Coco had trailed off again, the guilt was working away. "It's your house as much as ours, Aunt Coco. You know that. It's not as if you have to ask permission to invite anyone you like. It's simply that I think we should have—"

"No, no, it's inexcusable." Coco had blinked enough to have her eyes glistening nicely. "Really it was. I just don't know what to say. I feel terrible about the whole thing. I was only trying to help, you see, but—"

"It's nothing to worry about." C.C. reached out for her aunt's hand. "Nothing at all. It was just a little confusing at first. Look, why don't I make the tea, and you can sit with—him."

"That's so sweet of you, dear."

C.C. muttered something unintelligible as she walked down the hall.

"Congratulations," Trent murmured, sending Coco an amused glance. "That was one of the smoothest shuffles I've ever witnessed."

Coco beamed and tucked her arm through his. "Thank you. Now, why don't we go in and have that chat?" She steered him to a wing chair by the fireplace, knowing that the springs in the sofa were only a memory. "I must apologize for C.C. She has a very quick temper but a wonderful heart."

Trent inclined his head. "I'll have to take your word for it."

"Well, you're here and that's what matters." Pleased with herself, Coco sat across from him. "I know you'll find The Towers, and its history, fascinating."

He smiled, thinking he'd already found its occupants a fascination.

"My grandfather," she said, gesturing to a portrait of a dour-faced thin-lipped man above the ornate cherrywood mantel. "He built this house in 1904."

Trent glanced up at the disapproving eyes and lowered brows. "He looks...formidable," he said politely.

Coco gave a gay laugh. "Oh, indeed. And ruthless in his prime, so I'm told. I only remember Fergus Calhoun as a doddering old man who argued with shadows. They finally put him away in 1945 after he ried to shoot the butler for serving bad port. He was quite insane—Grandfather," she explained. "Not the butler."

"I...see."

"He lived another twelve years in the asylum, which put him well into his eighties. The Calhouns either have long lives or die tragically young." She crossed her long, sturdy legs. "I knew your father."

"My father?"

"Yes, indeed. Not well. We attended some of the same parties in our youth. I remember dancing with him once at a cotillion in Newport. He was dashingly handsome, fatally charming. I was quite smitten." She smiled. "You resemble him closely."

"He must have fumbled to let you slip through his fingers."

Pure feminine delight glowed in her eyes. "You're quite right," she said with a laugh. "How is Trenton?"

"He's well. I think if he had realized the connection, he wouldn't have passed this business on to me."

She lifted a brow. As a woman who followed the society and gossip pages religiously, she was well aware of the senior St. James's current messy divorce. "The last marriage didn't take?"

It was hardly a secret, but it made Trent uncomfortable just the same. "No. Should I give him your regards when I speak with him?"

"Please do." A sore point, she noted, and skimmed lightly over it. "How is it you ran into C.C.?"

Fate, he thought, and nearly said so. "I found myself in need of her services—or I should say my car needed them. I didn't immediately make the connection between C.C.'s Automovations and Catherine Calhoun."

"Who could blame you?" Coco said with a fluttering hand. "I hope she wasn't too, ah, intense."

"I'm still alive to talk about it. Obviously, your niece isn't convinced to sell."

"That's right." C.C. wheeled in a tea cart, steering it across the floor like a go-cart and stopping it with a rattle between the two chairs. "And it's going to take more than some slick operator from Boston to convince me.''

"Catherine, there is no excuse for rudeness."

"That's all right." Trent merely settled back. "I'm becoming used to it. Are all your nieces so... aggressive, Mrs. McPike?"

"Coco, please," she murmured. "They're all lovely women." As she lifted the teapot, she sent C.C. a warning glance. "Don't you have work, dear?"

"It can wait."

"But you only brought out service for two."

"I don't want anything." She plopped down on the arm of the sofa and folded her arms over her chest.

"Well then. Cream or lemon, Trenton?"

"Lemon, please."

Swinging one long, booted leg, C.C. watched them sip tea and exchange small talk. Useless talk, she thought nastily. He was the kind of man who had been trained from diapers on the proper way to sit in a parlor and discuss nothing.

Squash, polo, perhaps a round of golf. He probably had hands like a baby's. Beneath that tailored suit, his body would be soft and slow. Men like him didn't work, didn't sweat, didn't feel. He sat behind his desk all day, buying and selling, never once thinking of the lives he affected. Of the dreams and hopes he created or destroyed.

He wasn't going to mess with hers. He wasn't going to cover the much-loved and much-cracked plaster walls with drywall and a coat of slick paint. He wasn't going to turn the drafty old ballroom into a nightclub. He wasn't going to touch one board foot of her wormy rafters.

She would see to it. She would see to him.

It was quite a situation, Trent decided. He parried Coco's tea talk while the Amazon Queen, as he'd begun to think of C.C., sat on a sagging sofa, swinging a scarred boot and glaring daggers at him. Normally he would have politely excused himself, headed back to Boston to turn the whole business over to agents. But he hadn't faced a true challenge in a long time. This one, he mused, might be just what he needed to put him on track.

The place itself was an amazement—a crumbling one. From the outside it looked like a combination of English manor house and Dracula's castle. Towers and turrets of dour gray stone jutted into the sky. Gargoyles—one of which had been decapitated—grinned wickedly as they clung to parapets. All of this seemed to sit atop a proper two-story house of granite with neat porches and terraces. There was a pergola built along the seawall. The quick glimpse Trent had had of it had brought a Roman bathhouse to mind for reasons he couldn't fathom. As the lawns were uneven and multileveled, granite walls had been thrown up wherever they were terraced.

It should have been ugly. In fact, Trent thought it should have been hideous. Yet it wasn't. It was, in a baffling way, charming.

The way the window glass sparkled like lake water in the sun. Banks of spring flowers spread and nodded. Ivy rustled as it inched its patient way up those granite walls. It hadn't been difficult, even for a man with a pragmatic mind, to imagine the tea and garden parties. Women floating over the lawns in picture hats and organdy dresses, harp and violin music playing.

Then there was the view, which even on the short walk from his car to the front door had struck him breathless.

He could see why his father wanted it, and was willing to invest the hundreds of thousands of dollars it would take to renovate.

"More tea, Trenton?" Coco asked.

"No, thank you." He sent her a charming smile. "I wonder if I might have a tour of the house. What I've seen so far is fascinating."

C.C. gave a snort Coco pretended not to hear. "Of course, I'd be delighted to show you through." She rose and with her back to Trent wiggled her eyebrows at her niece. "C.C., shouldn't you be getting back?"

"No." She rose and, with an abrupt change of tactics, smiled. "I'll show Mr. St. James through, Aunt Coco. It's nearly time for the children to be home from school."

Coco glanced at the mantel clock, which had stopped weeks before at ten thirty-five. "Oh, well..."

"Don't worry about a thing." C.C. walked to the doorway and with an imperious gesture of her hand waved Trent along. "Mr. St. James?"

She started down the hall in front of him then up a floating staircase. "We'll start at the top, shall we?" Without glancing back, she continued on and up, certain Trent would start wheezing and panting by the third flight.

She was disappointed.

They climbed the final circular set that led to the highest tower. C.C. put her hand on the knob and her shoulder to the thick oak door. With a grunt and a hard shove, it creaked open.

"The haunted tower," she said grandly, and stepped inside amid the dust and echoes. The circular room was empty but for a few sturdy and fortunately empty mouse traps.

"Haunted?" Trent repeated, willing to play.

"My great-grandmother had her hideaway up here." As she spoke, C.C. moved over to the curved window. "It's said she would sit here, on this window seat, looking out to sea as she pined for her lover."

"Quite a view," Trent murmured. It was a dizzying drop down to the cliffs and the water that slapped and retreated. "Very dramatic."

"Oh, we're full of drama here. Great-Grandmama apparently couldn't bear the deceit any longer and threw herself out this very window." C.C. smiled smugly. "Now, on quiet nights you can hear her pacing this floor and weeping for her lost lover."

"That should add something to the brochure."

C.C. jammed her hands into her pockets. "I wouldn't think ghosts would be good for business."

"On the contrary." His lips curved. "Shall we move on?"

Tight-lipped, C.C. strode out of the room. Using both hands, she tugged on the knob, then dug in a bit and prepared to put her back into it. When Trent's hand closed over hers, she jolted as though she'd been scalded.

It felt as though she had.

"I can do it," she muttered. Her eyes widened as she felt his body brush hers. He brought his other arm around, caging her, trapping her hands under his. C.C.'s heart bounded straight into her throat, then back-flipped.

"It looks like a two-man job." With this, Trent gave a hard tug that brought the door to and C.C. back smartly against him.

They stood there a moment, like lovers looking out at a sunset. He caught himself drawing in the scent of her hair while his hands remained cupped over hers. It passed through his mind that she was quite an armful—an amazingly sexy armful—then she jumped like a rabbit, slamming back against the wall.

"It's warped." She swallowed, hoping to smother the squeak in her voice. "Everything around here is warped or broken or about to disintegrate. I don't know why you'd even consider buying it."

Her face was pale as water, Trent noted, making her eyes that much deeper. The panicked distress in them seemed more than a warped tower door warranted. "Doors can be repaired or replaced." Curious, he took a step toward her and watched her brace as if for a blow. "What's wrong with you?"

"Nothing." She knew if he touched her again she would go off like a rocket through what was left of the roof. "Nothing," she repeated. "If you want to see anything else, we'd better go down."

C.C. let out a long, slow breath as she followed him down the circular stairs. Her body was still throbbing oddly, as if she'd brushed a hand over a live wire. Not enough to get singed, she thought, just enough to let you know there was power.

She decided that gave her two reasons to get rid of Trenton St. James quickly.

She took him through the top floor, through the servants' wing, the storage rooms, making certain to point out any cracked plaster, dry rot, rodent damage. It pleased her that the air was chill, slightly damp and definitely musty. It was even more gratifying to see that his suit was sprinkled with dust and his shoes were rapidly losing their shine.

Trent peered into one room that was crowded with furniture boxes, broken crockery. "Has anyone gone through all this stuff?"

"Oh, we'll get around to it eventually." She watched a fat spider sneak away from the dim light. "Most of these rooms haven't been opened in fifty years—since my great-grandfather went insane."

"Fergus."

"Right. The family only uses the first two floors, and we patch things up as we have to." She ran her finger along an inch-wide crack in the wall. "I guess you could say if we don't see it, we don't worry about it. And the roof hasn't crashed down on our heads. Yet."

He turned to study her. "Have you ever thought about turning in your socket wrench for a real estate license?"

She only smiled. "There's more down this way." She particularly wanted to show him the room where she had tacked up plastic to cover the broken windows.

He walked with her, gingerly across a spot where two-by-fours had been nailed over a hole in the floor. A high arched door caught his eyes, and before C.C. could stop him, he had his hand on the knob.

"Where does this lead to?"

"Oh, nowhere," she began, and swore when he pulled it open. Fresh spring air rushed in. Trent stepped out onto the narrow stone terrace and turned toward the pie-shaped granite steps.

"I don't know how safe they are."

He flicked a glance over his shoulder. "A lot safer than the floor inside."

With an oath, C.C. gave up and climbed after him.

"Fabulous," he murmured as he paused on the wide passageway between turrets. "Really fabulous."

Which was exactly why C.C. hadn't wanted him to see it. She stood back with her hands in her pockets while he rested his palms on the waist-high stone wall and looked out.

He could see the deep blue waters of the bay with the boats gliding lightly over it. The valley, misty and mysterious, spread like a fairy tale. A gull, hardly more than a white blur, banked over the bay and soared out to sea.

"Incredible." The wind ruffled his hair as he followed the passage, down another flight, up one more. From here it was the Atlantic, wild and windy and wonderful. The sound of her ceaseless war on the rocks below echoed up like thunder.

He could see that there were doors leading back in at various intervals, but he wasn't interested in the interior just now. Someone, one of the family, he imagined, had set out chairs, tables, potted plants. Trent looked out over the roof of the pergola, to the tumbling rocks below.

"Spectacular." He turned to C.C. "Do you get used to it?"

She moved her shoulders. "No. You just get territorial."

"Understandable. I'm surprised any of you spend time inside."

With her hands still tucked in her pockets, she joined him at the wall. "It's not just the view. It's the fact that your family, generations of them, stood here. Just as the house has stood here, through time and wind and fire." Her face softened as she looked down. "The children are home."

Trent looked down to see two small figures race across the lawn toward the pergola. The sound of their laughter carried lightly on the wind.

"Alex and Jenny," she explained. "My sister Suzanna's children. They've stood here, too." She turned to him. "That means something."

"How does their mother feel about the sale?"

She looked away then as worry and guilt and frustration fought for control. "I'm sure you'll ask her yourself. But if you pressure her." Her head whipped around, hair flying. "If you pressure her in any way, you'll answer to me. I won't see her manipulated again."

"I have no intention of manipulating anyone."

She gave a bark of bitter laughter. "Men like you make a career out of manipulation. If you think you've happened across four helpless women, Mr. St. James, think again. The Calhouns can take care of themselves, and take care of their own."

"Undoubtedly, particularly if your sisters are as obnoxious as you."

C.C.'s eyes narrowed, her hands fisted. She would have moved in then and there for the kill, but her name was murmured quietly behind her.

Trent saw a woman step through one of the doors. She was as tall as C.C., but willowy, with a fragile aura that kicked Trent's protective instincts into gear before he was aware of it. Her hair was a pale and lustrous blond that waved to her shoulders. Her eyes were the deep blue of a midsummer sky and seemed calm and serene until you looked closer and saw the heartbreak beneath.

Despite the difference in coloring, there was a resemblance—the shape of the face and eyes and mouth—that made Trent certain he was meeting one of C.C.'s sisters.

"Suzanna." C.C. moved between her sister and Trent, as if to shield. Suzanna's mouth curved, a look that was both amused and impatient.

"Aunt Coco asked me to come up." She laid a hand on C.C.'s arm, soothing her protector. "You must be Mr. St. James."

"Yes." He accepted her offered hand and was surprised to find it hard and callused and strong.

"I'm Suzanna Calhoun Dumont. You'll be staying with us for a few days?"

"Yes. Your aunt was kind enough to invite me."

"Shrewd enough," Suzanna corrected with a smile as she put an arm around her sister. "I take it C.C.'s given you a partial tour."

"A fascinating one."

"I'll be glad to continue it from here." Her fingers pressed lightly but with clear meaning into C.C.'s arm. "Aunt Coco could use some help downstairs."

"He doesn't need to see any more now," C.C. argued. "You look tired."

"Not a bit. But I will be if Aunt Coco sends me all over the house looking for the Wedgwood turkey platter."

"All right then." She sent Trent a last, fulminating glance. "We aren't finished."

"Not by a long shot," he agreed, and smiled to himself as she slammed back inside. "Your sister has quite an . . . outgoing personality."

"She's a fire-eater," Suzanna said. "We all are, given the right circumstances. The Calhoun curse." She glanced over at the sound of her children laughing. "This isn't an easy decision, Mr. St. James, one way or the other. Nor is it, for any of us, a business one."

"I've gathered that. For me it has to be a business one."

She knew too well that for some men business came first, and last. "Then I suppose we'd better take it one step at a time." She opened the door that C.C. had slammed shut. "Why don't I show you where you'll be staying?"

Chapter Three

"So, what's he like?" Lilah Calhoun crossed her long legs, anchoring her ankles on one arm of the couch and pillowing her head on the other. The half-dozen bracelets on her arm jingled as she gestured toward C.C. "Honey, I've told you, screwing your face up that way causes nothing but wrinkles and bad vibes."

"If you don't want me to screw my face up, don't ask me about him."

"Okay, I'll ask Suzanna." She shifted her sea-green eyes toward her older sister. "Let's have it."

"Attractive, well mannered and intelligent."

"So's a cocker spaniel," Lilah put in, and sighed. "And here I was hoping for a pit bull. How long do we get to keep him?"

"Aunt Coco's a little vague on the particulars." Suzanna sent both of her sisters an amused look. "Which means she's not saying."

"Mandy might be able to pry something out of her." Lilah wiggled her bare toes and shut her eyes. She was the kind of woman who felt there was something intrinsically wrong with anyone who stretched out on a couch and didn't nap. "Suze, have the kids been through here today?"

"Only ten or fifteen times. Why?"

"I think I'm lying on a fire engine."

"I think we ought to get rid of him." C.C. rose and, to keep her restless hands busy, began to lay a fire.

"Suzanna said you already tried to throw him off the parapet."

"No," Suzanna corrected. "I said I stopped her before she thought to throw him off the parapet." She rose to hand C.C. the fireplace matches she'd forgotten. "And while I agree it's awkward to have him here while we're all so undecided, it's done. The least we can do is give him a chance to say his piece."

"Always the peacemaker," Lilah said sleepily, and missed Suzanna's quick wince. "Well, it might be a moot point now that he's gone through the place. My guess is that he'll be making some clever excuse and zooming back to Boston."

"The sooner the better," C.C. muttered, watching the flames begin to lick at the apple wood.

"I've been dismissed," Amanda announced. She hurried into the room as she hurried everywhere. Pushing a hand through her chin-length honey-brown hair, she perched on the arm of a chair. "She's not talking, either." Amanda's busy hands tugged at the hem of her trim business suit. "But I know she's up to something, something more than real estate transactions."

"Aunt Coco's always up to something." Suzanna moved automatically to the old Belker cabinet to pour her sister a glass of mineral water. "She's happiest when she's scheming."

"That may be true. Thanks," she added, taking the glass. "But I get nervous when I can't get past her guard." Thoughtful, she sipped, then swept her gaze over her sisters. "She's using the Limoges china."

"The Limoges?" Lilah pushed up on her elbows. "We haven't used that since Suzanna's engagement party." And could have bitten her tongue. "Sorry."

"Don't be silly." Suzanna brushed the apology away. "She hasn't entertained much in the past couple of years. I'm sure she's missed it. She's probably just excited to have company."

"He's not company," C.C. put in. "He's nothing but a pain in the—"

"Mr. St. James." Suzanna rose quickly, cutting off the finale of her sister's opinion.

"Trent, please." He smiled at her, then with some wryness at C.C.

It was quite a tableau, he thought, and had enjoyed it for perhaps a minute before Suzanna had seen him in the doorway. The Calhoun women together, and separately, made a picture any man still breathing had to appreciate. Long, lean and leggy, they sat, stood or sprawled around the room.

Suzanna stood with her back to the window, so that the last lights of the spring evening haloed around her hair. He would have said she was relaxed but for that trace of sadness in her eyes.

The one on the sofa was definitely relaxed—and all but asleep. She wore a long, flowered skirt that reached almost to her bare feet and regarded him through dreamy amused eyes as she pushed back a curling mass of waist-length red hair.

Another sat perched on the arm of a chair as if he would spring up and into action at the sound of a bell only she could hear. Sleek, slick and professional, he thought at first glance. Her eyes weren't dreamy or sad, but simply calculating.

Then there was C.C. She'd been sitting on the stone hearth, chin on her hands, brooding like some modern-day Cinderella. But she had risen quickly, defensively, he noted, to stand poker straight with the fire behind her. This wasn't a woman who would sit patiently for a prince to fit a glass slipper on her foot.

He imagined she'd kick him smartly in the shins or somewhere more painful if he attempted it.

"Ladies," he said, but his eyes were on C.C. without him even being aware of it. He couldn't resist the slight nod in her direction. "Catherine."

"Let me introduce you," Suzanna said quickly. "Trenton St. James, my sisters, Amanda and Lilah. Why don't I fix you a drink while you—"

The rest of the offer was drowned out by a war whoop and storming feet. Like twin whirlwinds, Alex and Jenny barreled into the room. It was Trent's misfortune that he happened to be standing in the line of fire. They slammed into him like two missiles and sent him tumbling to the couch on top of Lilah.

She only laughed and said she was pleased to meet him.

"I'm so sorry." Suzanna collared each child and sent Trent a sympathetic glance. "Are you all right?"

"Yes." He untangled himself and rose.

"These are my children, Disaster and Calamity."
She kept a firm maternal arm around each. "Apologize."

"Sorry," they told him. Alex, a few inches taller
than his sister looked up from under a mop of dark
hair.

"We didn't see you."

"Didn't," Jenny agreed, and smiled winningly.

Suzanna decided to go into the lecture about
storming into rooms later and steered them both toward the door. "Go ask Aunt Coco if dinner's ready.
Walk!" she added firmly but without hope.

Before anyone could pick up the threads of a conversation, there was a loud, echoing boom.

"Oh, Lord," Amanda said into her glass. "She's
dragged out the gong again."

"That means dinner." If there was one thing Lilah
moved quickly for, it was food. She rose, tucked her
arm through Trent's and beamed up at him. "I'll show
you the way. Tell me, Trent, what are your views on
astral projection?"

"Ah..." He sent a glance over his shoulder and saw
C.C. grinning.

Aunt Coco had outdone herself. The china
gleamed. What was left of the Georgian silver that had
been a wedding present to Bianca and Fergus Calhoun glittered. Under the fantasy light of the Water-
ford chandelier the rack of lamb glistened. Before any
of her nieces could comment, she dived cleanly into
polite conversation.

"We're dining formal style, Trenton. So much more
cozy. I hope your room is suitable."

"It's fine, thank you." It was, he thought, big as a barn, drafty, with a hole the size of a man's fist in the ceiling. But the bed was wide and soft as a cloud. And the view... "I can see some islands from my window."

"The Porcupine islands," Lilah put in, and passed him a silver basket of dinner rolls.

Coco watched them all like a hawk. She wanted to see some chemistry, some heat. Lilah was flirting with him, but she couldn't be too hopeful about that. Lilah flirted with men in general, and she wasn't paying any more attention to Trent than she did to the boy who bagged groceries in the market.

No, there was no spark there. On either side. One down, she thought philosophically, three to go.

"Trenton, did you know that Amanda is also in the hotel business? We're all so proud of our Mandy." She looked down the rosewood table at her niece. "She's quite a businesswoman."

"I'm assistant manager of the BayWatch, down in the village." Amanda's smile was both cool and friendly, the same she would give to any harried tourist at checkout time. "It's not on the scale of any of your hotels, but we do very well during the season. I heard you're adding an underground shopping complex to the St. James Atlanta."

Coco frowned into her wine as they discussed hotels. Not only was there not a spark, there wasn't even a weak glow. When Trent passed Amanda the mint jelly and their hands brushed, there was no breathless pause, no meeting of the eyes. Amanda had already turned to giggle with little Jenny and mop up spilled milk.

Ah, there! Coco thought triumphantly. Trent had grinned at Alex when the boy complained that brussels sprouts were disgusting. So, he had a weakness for children.

"You don't have to eat them," Suzanna told her suspicious son as he poked through his scalloped potatoes to make sure nothing green was hidden inside. "Personally, I've always thought they looked like shrunken heads."

"They do, kinda." The idea appealed to him, as his mother had known it would. He speared one, stuck it into his mouth and grinned. "I'm a cannibal. Uga bugga."

"Darling boy," Coco said faintly. "Suzanna's done such a marvelous job of mothering. She seems to have a green thumb with children as well as flowers. All the gardens are our Suzanna's work."

"Uga bugga," Alex said again as he popped another imaginary head into his mouth.

"Here you go, little creep." C.C. rolled her vegetables onto his plate. "There's a whole passel of missionaries."

"I want some, too," Jenny complained, then beamed at Trent when he passed her the bowl.

Coco put a hand to her breast. Who would have guessed it? she thought. Her Catherine. The baby of her babies. While the dinner conversation bounced around her, she sat back with a quiet sigh. She couldn't be mistaken. Why, when Trent had looked at her little girl—and she at him—there hadn't just been a spark. There had been a sizzle.

C.C. was scowling, it was true, but it was such a *passionate* scowl. And Trent had smirked, but it was such a *personal* smirk. Positively intimate, Coco decided.

Sitting there, watching them, as Alex devoured his little decapitated heads, and Lilah and Amanda argued over the possibility of life on other planets, Coco could almost hear the loving thoughts C.C. and Trent sent out to each other.

Arrogant, self-important jerk.

Rude, bad-tempered brat.

Who the hell does he think he is, sitting at the table as if he already owned it?

A pity she doesn't have a personality to match her looks.

Coco smiled fondly at them while the "Wedding March" hummed through her head. Like a general plotting strategy, she waited until after coffee and dessert to spring her next offensive.

"C.C., why don't you show Trenton the gardens?"

"What?" She looked up from her friendly fight with Alex over the last bite of her Black Forest cake.

"The gardens," Coco repeated. "There's nothing like a little fresh air after a meal. And the flowers are exquisite in the moonlight."

"Let Suzanna take him."

"Sorry." Suzanna was already gathering a heavy-eyed Jenny into her arms. "I've got to get these two washed up and ready for bed."

"I don't see why—" C.C. broke off at the arched look from her aunt. "Oh, all right." She rose. "Come on then," she said to Trent and started out without him.

"It was a lovely meal, Coco. Thank you."

"My pleasure." She beamed, imagining whispered words and soft, secret kisses. "Enjoy the gardens."

Trent walked out of the terrace doors to find C.C. standing, tapping a booted foot on the stone. It was time, he thought, that someone taught the green-eyed witch a lesson in manners.

"I don't know anything about flowers," she told him.

"Or about simple courtesy."

Her chin angled. "Now listen, buddy."

"No, you listen, buddy." His hand snaked out and snagged her arm. "Let's walk. The children might still be within earshot, and I don't think they're ready to hear any of this."

He was stronger than she'd imagined. He pulled her along, ignoring the curses she tossed out under her breath. They were off the terrace and onto one of the meandering paths that wound around the side of the house. Daffodils and hyacinths nodded along the verge.

He stopped beneath an arbor where wisteria would bloom in another month. C.C. wasn't certain if the roar in her head was the sound of the sea or her own ragged temper.

"Don't you ever do that again." She lifted a hand to rub where his fingers had dug. "You may be able to push people around in Boston, but not here. Not with me or any of my family."

He paused, hoping and failing to get a grip on his own temper. "If you knew me, or what I do, you'd know I don't make a habit of pushing anyone around."

"I know exactly what you do."

"Foreclose on widows and orphans? Grow up, C.C."

She set her teeth. "You can see the gardens on your own. I'm going in."

He merely shifted to block her path. In the moonlight, her eyes glowed like a cat's. When she lifted her hands to shove him aside, he clamped his fingers onto her wrists. In the brief tug-of-war that followed, he noted—irrelevantly he assured himself—that her skin was the color of fresh cream and almost as soft.

"We're not finished." His voice had an edge that was no longer coated with a polite veneer. "You'll have to learn that when you're deliberately rude, and deliberately insulting, there's a price."

"You want an apology?" she all but spat at him. "Okay. I'm sorry I don't have anything to say to you that isn't rude or insulting."

He smiled, surprising both of them. "You're quite a piece of work, Catherine Colleen Calhoun. For the life of me I can't figure out why I'm trying to be reasonable with you."

"Reasonable?" She didn't spit the word this time, but growled it. "You call it reasonable to drag me around, manhandle me—"

"If you call this manhandling, you've led a very sheltered life."

Her complexion went from creamy white to bright pink. "My life is none of your concern."

"Thank God."

Her fingers flexed then balled into fists. She hated the fact, loathed it, that her pulse was hammering double time under his grip. "Will you let me go?"

"Only if you promise not to take off running." He could see himself chasing her, and the image was both embarrassing and appealing.

"I don't run from anyone."

"Spoken like a true Amazon," he murmured, and released her. Only quick reflexes had him dodging the fist she aimed at his nose. "I should have taken that into account, I suppose. Have you ever considered intelligent conversation?"

"I don't have anything to say to you." She was ashamed to have struck out at him and furious that she'd missed. "If you want to talk, go suck up to Aunt Coco some more." In a huff, she plopped down on the small stone bench under the arbor. "Better yet, go back to Boston and flog one of your underlings."

"I can do that anytime." He shook his head and, certain he was taking his life in his hands, sat beside her.

There were azaleas and geraniums threatening to burst into bloom around them. It should, he thought, have been a peaceful place. But as he sat, smelling the tender fragrance of the earliest spring blooms mixed with the scent of the sea, listening to some night bird call its mate, he thought that no boardroom had ever been so tense or hostile.

"I wonder where you developed such a high opinion of me." And why, he added to himself, it seemed to matter.

"You come here—"

"By invitation."

"Not mine." She tossed back her head. "You come in your big car and your dignified suit, ready to sweep my home out from under me."

"I came," he corrected, "to get a firsthand look at a piece of property. No one, least of all me, can force you to sell."

But he was wrong, she thought miserably. There were people who could force them to sell. The people who collected the taxes, the utility bills, the mortgage they'd been forced to take out. All of her frustration, and her fear, over every collection agency centered on the man beside her.

"I know your type," she muttered. "Born rich and above the common man. Your only goal in life is to make more money, regardless of who is affected or trampled over. You have big parties and summer houses and mistresses named Fawn."

Wisely he swallowed the chuckle. "I've never even known a woman named Fawn."

"Oh, what does it matter?" She rose to pace the path. "Kiki, Vanessa, Ava, it's all the same."

"If you say so." She looked, he was forced to admit, magnificent, striding up and down the path with the moonlight shooting around her like white fire. The tug of attraction annoyed him more than a little, but he continued to sit. There was a deal to be done, he reminded himself. And C. C. Calhoun was the foremost stumbling block.

So he would be patient, Trent told himself, and wily and find the hook. "Just how is it you know so much about my type?"

"Because my sister was married to one of you."

"Baxter Dumont."

"You know him?" Then she shook her head and jammed her hands into her pockets. "Stupid question. You probably play golf with him every Wednesday."

"No, actually our acquaintance is only slight. I do know of him, and his family. I'm also aware that he and your sister have been divorced for a year or so."

"He made her life hell, scraped away her self-esteem, then dumped her and his children for some little French pastry. And because he's a big-shot lawyer from a big-shot family, she's left with nothing but a miserly child-support check that comes late every month."

"I'm sorry for what happened to your sister." He rose as well. His voice was no longer sharp but fatalistic. "Marriage is often the least pleasant of all business transactions. But Baxter Dumont's behavior doesn't mean that every member of every prominent Boston family is unethical or immoral."

"They all look the same from where I'm standing."

"Then maybe you should change positions. But you won't, because you're too hardheaded and opinionated."

"Just because I'm smart enough to see through you."

"You know nothing about me, and we both know that you took an uncanny dislike to me before you even knew my name."

"I didn't like your shoes?"

That stopped him. "I beg your pardon?"

"You heard me." She folded her arms and realized she was starting to enjoy herself. "I didn't like your shoes." She flicked a glance down at them. "I still don't."

"That explains everything."

"I didn't like your tie, either." She poked a finger on it, missing the quick flare in his eyes. "Or your fancy gold pen." She tapped a fist lightly at his breast pocket.

He studied her jeans, worn through at the knees, her T-shirt and scuffed boots. "This from an obvious fashion expert."

"You're the one out of place here, Mr. St. James III."

He took a step closer. C.C.'s lips curved in a challenging smile. "And I suppose you dress like a man because you haven't figured out how to act like a woman."

It was a bull's-eye, but the dart point only pricked her temper. "Just because I know how to stand up for myself instead of swooning at your feet doesn't make me less of a woman."

"Is that what you call this?" He wrapped his fingers around her forearms. "Standing up for yourself?"

"That's right. I—" She broke off when he tugged her closer. Their bodies bumped. Trent watched the temper in her eyes deepen to confusion.

"What do you think you're doing?"

"Testing the theory." He looked down at her mouth. Her lips were full, just parted. Very tempting. Why hadn't he noticed that before? he wondered vaguely. That big, insulting mouth of hers was incredibly tempting.

"Don't you dare." She meant it to come out as an order, but her voice shook.

His eyes came back to hers and held. "Afraid?"

The question was just the one to stiffen her spine. "Of course not. It's just that I'd rather be kissed by a rabid skunk."

She started to pull back, then found herself tight against him, eyes and mouth lined up, warm breath mingling. He hadn't intended to kiss her—certainly not—until she'd thrown that last insult in his face.

"You never know when to quit, Catherine. It's a flaw that's going to get you in trouble, starting now."

She hadn't expected his mouth to be so hot, so hard, so hungry. She had thought the kiss would be sophisticated and bland. Easily resisted, easily forgotten. But she had been wrong. Dangerously wrong. Kissing him was like sliding into molten silver. Even as she gasped for air, he heightened the kiss, plunging his tongue deep, taunting, tormenting, teasing hers. She tried to shake her head but succeeded only in changing the angle. The hands that had reached for his shoulders in protest slid possessively around his neck.

He'd thought to teach her a lesson—about what he'd forgotten. But he learned. He learned that some women—this woman—could be strong and soft, frustrating and delightful, all at once. As the waves crashed far below, he felt himself battered by the unexpected. And the unwanted.

He thought, foolishly, that he could feel the starlight on her skin, taste the moondust on her lips. The groan he heard, vibrating low, was his own.

He lifted his head, shaking it, as if to clear the fog that had settled over his brain. He could see her eyes, staring up at his—dark, dazed.

"I beg your pardon." Stunned by his action, he released her so quickly that she stumbled back even as her hands slid away from him. "That was completely inexcusable."

She said nothing, could say nothing. Feelings, too many of them, clogged in her throat. Instead she made a helpless gesture with her hands that made him feel like a lower form of life.

"Catherine...believe me, I don't make a habit of—" He had to stop and clear his dry throat. Lord, he wanted to do it again, he realized. He wanted to kiss the breath from her as she stood there, looking lost and helpless. And beautiful. "I'm terribly sorry. It won't happen again."

"I'd like you to leave me alone." Never in her life had she been more moved. Or more devastated. He had just opened up a door to some secret world, then slammed it again in her face.

"All right." He had to stop himself from reaching out to touch her hair. He started back down the path toward the house. When he looked back, she was still standing as he had left her, staring into the shadows, with moonlight showering her.

His name is Christian. I have found myself walking along the cliffs again and again, hoping for a few words with him. I tell myself it's because of my fascination with art, not the artist. It could be true. It must be true.

I am a married woman and mother of three. And though Fergus is not the romantic husband of my girlish dreams, he is a good provider, and sometimes kind. Perhaps there is some part of me, some small defiant part that wishes I had not bent to my parents' insistence that I make a good and proper marriage.

But this is foolishness, for the deed has been done for more than four years.

It's disloyal to compare Fergus with a man I hardly know. Yet here, in my private journal, I must be allowed this indulgence. While Fergus thinks only of business, the next deal or dollar, Christian speaks of dreams and images and poetry.

How my heart has yearned for just a little poetry.

While Fergus, with his cool and careless generosity, gave me the emeralds on the day of Ethan's birth, Christian once offered me a wildflower. I have kept it, pressing it here between these pages. How much lovelier I would feel wearing it than those cold and heavy gems.

We have spoken of nothing intimate, nothing that could be considered improper. Yet I know it is. The way he looks at me, smiles, speaks, is gloriously improper. The way I look for him on these bright summer afternoons while my babies nap is not the action of a proper wife. The way my heart drums in my breast when I see him is disloyalty in itself.

Today I sat upon a rock and watched him wield his brush, bringing those pink and gray rocks, that blue, blue water to life on canvas. There was a boat gliding along, so free, so solitary. For a moment I pictured the two of us there, faces to the wind. I don't understand why I have these thoughts, but while they remained with me, clear as crystal, I asked his name.

"Christian," he said. "Christian Bradford. And you are Bianca."

The way he said my name—as if it had never been said before. I will never forget it. I toyed with the wild grass that pushed itself through the cracks in the rocks.

With my eyes cast down, I asked him why his wife never came to watch him work.

"I have no wife," he told me. "And art is my only mistress."

It was wrong for my heart to swell so at his words. Wrong of me to smile, yet I smiled. And he in return. If fate had dealt differently with me, if time and place could have been altered in some way, I could have loved him.

I think I would have had no choice but to love him.

As if we both knew this, we began to talk of inconsequential matters. But when I rose, knowing my time here was at an end for the day, he bent over and plucked up a tiny spike of golden heather and slipped it into my hair. For a moment, his fingers hovered over my cheek and his eyes were on mine. Then he stepped away and bid me good day.

Now I sit with the lamp low as I write, listening to Fergus's voice rumble as he instructs his valet next door. He will not come to me tonight, and I find myself grateful. I have given him three children, two sons and a daughter. By providing him with an heir, I have done my duty, and he does not often find the need to come to my bed. I am, like the children, to exist to be well dressed and well mannered, and to be presented at the proper occasions—like a good claret—for his guests.

It is not much to ask, I suppose. It is a good life, one I should be content with. Perhaps I was content, until that day I first walked along the cliffs.

So tonight, I will sleep alone in my bed, and dream of a man who is not my husband.

Chapter Four

When you couldn't sleep, the best thing to do was get up. That's what C.C. told herself as she sat at the kitchen table, watching the sunrise and drinking her second cup of coffee.

She had a lot on her mind, that was all. Bills, the dyseptic Oldsmobile that was first on her schedule that morning, bills, an upcoming dentist appointment. More bills. Trenton St. James was far down on her list of concerns. Somewhere below a potential cavity and just ahead of a faulty exhaust system.

She certainly wasn't losing any sleep over him. And a kiss, that ridiculous—*accident* was the best term she could use to describe it—wasn't even worth a moment's thought.

Yet she had thought of little else throughout the long, sleepless night.

She was acting as though she'd never been kissed before, C.C. berated herself. And, of course, she had, starting with Denny Dinsmore, who had planted the first sloppy mouth-to-mouth on her after their eighth-grade Valentine's dance.

Naturally there had been no comparison between Denny's fumbling yet sincere attempt and the stunning expertise of Trent's. Which only proved, C.C. decided as she scowled into her coffee, that Trent had spent a large part of his life with his lips slapped up against some woman's. Lots of women's.

It had been a rotten thing to do, she thought now. Particularly in the middle of what had been becoming a very satisfactory argument. Men like Trent didn't know how to fight fair, with wit and words and good honest fury. They were taught how to dominate, by whatever manner worked.

Well, it had worked, she thought, running a finger-tip over her lips. Damn him and the horse he rode in on. It had worked like a charm, because for one moment, one brief, trembling moment she had felt something fine and lovely—something more than the exciting press of his mouth on hers, more than the possessive grip of his hands.

It had been inside her, beneath the panic and the pleasure, beyond the whirl of sensation—a glow, warm and golden, like a lamp in the window on a stormy night.

Then he had turned off that lamp, with one quick, careless flick, leaving her in the dark again.

She could have hated him for that alone, C.C. thought miserably, if she hadn't already had enough to hate him for.

"Hey, kid." Lilah breezed through the doorway, tidy in her park service khakis. Her mass of hair was in a neat braid down her back. Swinging at each ear was a trio of amber crystal balls. "You're up early."

"Me?" C.C. forgot her own mood long enough to stare. "Are you my sister or some clever imposter?"

"You be the judge."

"Must be an imposter. Lilah Maeve Calhoun's never up before eight o'clock, which is exactly twenty minutes before she has to rush out of the house to be five minutes late for work."

"God, I hate to be so predictable. My horoscope," Lilah told her as she rooted through the refrigerator. "It said that I should rise early today and contemplate the sunrise."

"So how was it?" C.C. asked as her sister brought a cold can of soda and a wicked slice of the Black Forest cake to the table.

"Pretty spectacular as sunrises go." Lilah shoveled cake into her mouth. "What's your excuse?"

"Couldn't sleep."

"Anything to do with the stranger at the end of the hall?"

C.C. wrinkled her nose and filched a cherry from Lilah's plate. "Guys like that don't bother me."

"Guys like that were created to bother women, and thank God for it. So..." Lilah stretched her legs out to rest her feet on an empty chair. The kitchen faucet was leaking again, but she liked the sound of it. "What's the story?"

"I didn't say there was a story."

"You don't have to say, it's all over your face."

"I just don't like him being here, that's all." Evading, C.C. rose to take her cup to the sink. "It's like we're already being pushed out of our own home. I know we've discussed selling, but it was all so vague and down some long, dark road." She turned back to her sister. "Lilah, what are we going to do?"

"I don't know." Lilah's eyes clouded. It was one of the few things she couldn't prevent herself from worrying about. Home and family, they were her weaknesses. "I guess we could sell some more of the crystal, and there's the silver."

"It would break Aunt Coco's heart to sell the silver."

"I know. But we may have to go piece by piece—or make the big move." She scooped up some more cake. "As much as I hate to say it, we're going to have to think hard, and practically, and seriously."

"But, Lilah, a hotel?"

Lilah merely shrugged. "I don't have any deep, moral problem with that. The house was built by crazy old Fergus to entertain platoons of guests, with all kinds of people racing around to serve meals and tidy linens. It seems to me that a hotel just about suits its original purpose." She gave a long sigh at C.C.'s expression. "You know I love the place as much as you do."

"I know."

What Lilah didn't add was that it would break her heart to have to sell it but that she was prepared to do what was best for the family.

"We'll give the gorgeous Mr. St. James a couple more days, then have a family meeting." She offered

C.C. a bolstering smile. "The four of us together can't go wrong."

"I hope you're right."

"Honey, I'm always right—that's my little cross to bear." She took a swig of the sugar-ladened soft drink. "Now, why don't you tell me what kept you up all night?"

"I just did."

"No." Head cocked, she waved her fork at C.C. "Don't forget Lilah knows all and sees all—and what she doesn't she finds out. So spill it."

"Aunt Coco made me take him out in the garden."

"Yeah." Lilah grinned. "She's a wily old devil. I figured she was plotting some romance. Moonlight, flowers, the distant lap of water on rocks. Did it work?"

"We had a fight."

Lilah nodded, giving a go-ahead signal with her hand as she sipped. "That's a good start. About the house?"

"That..." C.C. began to pluck dried leaves from a withered philodendron. "And things."

"Like?"

"Names of mistresses," C.C. muttered. "Prominent Boston families. His shoes."

"An eclectic argument. My favorite kind. And then?"

C.C. jammed her hands into her pockets. "He kissed me."

"Ah, the plot thickens." She had Coco's love of gossip and, leaning forward, cradled her chin on her hands. "So, how was it? He's got a terrific mouth—I noticed it right off."

"So kiss him yourself."

After thinking it over a moment, Lilah shook her head—not without some regret. "Nope, terrific mouth or not, he's not my type. Anyway, you've already locked lips with him, so tell me. Was he good?"

"Yeah," C.C. said grudgingly. "I guess you could say that."

"Like on a scale of one to ten?"

The chuckle escaped before C.C. realized she was laughing. "I wasn't exactly thinking about a rating system at the time."

"Better and better." Lilah licked her fork clean. "So, he kissed you and it was pretty good. Then what?"

Humor vanished as C.C. blew out a long breath. "He apologized."

Lilah stared, then slowly, deliberately set down her fork. "He what?"

"Apologized—very properly for his inexcusable behavior, and promised it wouldn't happen again. The jerk." C.C. crumbled the dead leaves in her hand. "What kind of a man thinks a woman wants an apology after she's been kissed boneless?"

Lilah only shook her head. "Well, the way I see it, there are three choices. He *is* a jerk, he's been trained to be overly polite, or he was incapable of thinking rationally."

"I vote for jerk."

"Hmm. I'm going to have to think about this." She drummed her cerise-tipped fingers on the table. "Maybe I should do his chart."

"Whatever sign his moon is in, I still vote for jerk." C.C. walked over to kiss Lilah's cheek. "Thanks. Gotta go."

"C.C." She waited until her sister turned back. "He has nice eyes. When he smiles, he has very nice eyes."

Trent wasn't smiling when he finally managed to escape from The Towers that afternoon. Coco had insisted on giving him a tour of the cellars, every damp inch, then had trapped him with photo albums for two hours.

It had been amusing to look at baby pictures of C.C., to view, through snapshots, her growing up from toddler to woman. She had been incredibly cute in pigtails and a missing tooth.

During the second hour, his alarm bells had sounded. Coco had begun to pump him none too subtly about his views on marriage, children, relationships. It was then he'd realized that behind Coco's soft, misty eyes ticked a sharp, calculating brain.

She wasn't trying to sell the house but to auction off one of her nieces. And apparently C.C. was the front-runner, with him preselected as the highest bidder. Well, the Calhoun women were in for a rude awakening, Trent determined. They were going to have to look elsewhere on the marriage market for a suitable candidate—and good luck to him.

And the St. Jameses would have the house, Trent promised himself. By damn they would, with no strings or wedding veils attached.

He started down the steep, winding drive in a controlled fury. When he caught the sound of his own voice as he muttered to himself, Trent decided that he would take a long, calming drive. Perhaps to Acadia National Park where Lilah worked as a naturalist. Divide and conquer, he thought. He would seek out each of the women in their own work space and rattle their beautiful chains.

Lilah seemed to be receptive, he thought. Any one of them would be more so that C.C. Amanda appeared to be sensible. He was certain Suzanna was a reasonable woman.

What had gone wrong with sister number four?

But he found himself heading down to the village, past Suzanna's fledgling landscape and garden business, past the BayWatch Hotel. When he drove up to C.C.'s garage, he told himself that was what he'd meant to do all along.

He would start with her, the sharpest thorn in his side. And when he was done, she would have no illusions about trapping him into marriage.

Hank was climbing into the tow truck as Trent climbed out of the BMW. "'Lo." Grinning, Hank pulled on the brim of his gray cap. "Boss's inside. Got us a nice fender bender over at the visitor's center."

"Congratulations."

"Ayah, we've been needing a little bodywork 'round here. Now, once the season picks up, business'll boom." Hank slammed the door then leaned his head out of the window, disposed to chat.

For some reason, Trent found himself noticing the boy—really noticing him. He was young, probably about twenty, with a round, open face, a thick downeast accent and a shock of straw-colored hair that shot out in all directions.

"Have you worked for C.C. long?"

"Since she bought the place from old Pete. That'll be, ah, three years. Ayah. Three years, nearly. She wouldn't hire me till I finished high school. Funny that way."

"Is she?"

"Once she gets a bee in her bonnet ain't no shaking it loose." He nodded toward the garage. "She's a might touchy today."

"Is that unusual?"

Hank chuckled and switched the radio on high. "Can't say she's all bark and no bite, 'cause I've seen her bite a time or two. See ya."

"Sure."

When Trent walked in, C.C. was buried to the waist under the hood of a late-model sedan. She had the radio on again, but this time it was her hips rather than her boots keeping time.

"Excuse me," Trent began, then remembered they had been through that routine before. He walked up and tapped her smartly on the shoulder.

"If you'd just..." But she turned her head only enough to see the tie. It wasn't maroon today, but navy. Still, she was certain of its owner. "What do you want?"

"I believe it was a lube job."

"Oh." She went back to replacing spark plugs. "Well, leave it outside, put the key on the bench, and I'll get to it. It should be ready by six."

"Do you always do business so casually?"

"Yeah."

"If you don't mind, I think I'll hold on to my keys until you're less distracted."

"Suit yourself." Two minutes passed in humming silence broken only by the radio's prediction of thunderstorms that evening. "Look, if you're just going to stand around, why don't you do something useful? Get in and start her up."

"Start her up?"

"Yeah, you know. Turn the key, pump the gas." She cocked her head up and blew at her bangs. "Think you can handle it?"

"Probably." It wasn't exactly what he'd had in mind, but Trent walked around to the driver's side. He noted that there was a car seat strapped in the front, and something pink and gooey on the carpet. He slid in and turned the key. The engine turned over and purred, quite nicely, he thought. Apparently C.C. thought differently.

Taking up her timing light, she began to make adjustments.

"It sounds fine," Trent pointed out.

"No, there's a miss."

"How can you hear anything with the radio blasting?"

"How can you not hear it? Better," she murmured. "Better."

Curious, he got out to lean over her shoulder. "What are you doing?"

"My job." Her shoulders moved irritably, as if there were an itch between the blades. "Back off, will you?"

"I'm only expressing normal curiosity." Without thinking, he set a hand lightly on her back and leaned farther in. C.C. jolted, felt a flash of pain then swore like a sailor.

"Let me see." He grabbed the hand she was busy shaking.

"It's nothing. Take off, will you? If you hadn't been in my way, my hand wouldn't have slipped."

"Stop dancing around and let me see." He took a firm grip on her wrist and examined her scraped knuckles. The faint well of blood beneath the engine grease caused him a sharp and ridiculous sense of guilt. "You'll need something on this."

"It's just a scratch." God, why wouldn't he let go of her hand? "What I need to do is finish this job."

"Don't be a baby," he said mildly. "Where's the first-aid kit?"

"It's in the bathroom, and I can do it myself."

Ignoring her, he kept hold of her wrist as he walked around to shut the engine off. "Where's the bathroom?"

She jerked her head toward the hallway that separated the garage from the office. "If you'd just leave your keys—"

"You said it was my fault you hurt your hand, so I'll take the responsibility."

"I wish you'd stop pulling me around," she said as he hauled her toward the hallway.

"Then keep up." He pushed open a door into a white-tiled bathroom the size of a broom closet. Ignoring her protests, he held C.C.'s hand under a spray of cool water. The dimensions of the room had them standing hip to hip. They both did their level best to ignore that as he took the soap and, with surprising gentleness, began to clean her hand. "It isn't deep," he said, annoyed that his throat was dry.

"I told you, it's just a scratch."

"Scratches get infected."

"Yes, doctor."

With a retort on the tip of his tongue, he glanced up. She looked so cute, he thought, with grease on her nose and her mouth in a five-year-old's pout. "I'm sorry," he heard himself say, and the petulance faded from her eyes.

"It wasn't your fault." Wanting something to do, she opened the mirrored cabinet over the sink for the first-aid kit. "I can take care of it, really."

"I like to finish what I start." He took the kit from her and found the antiseptic. "I guess I should say this is going to sting."

"I already know it stings." C.C. let out a little hiss as he swabbed the cut. Automatically she leaned over to blow on the heat, just as he did the same. Their heads bumped smartly. Rubbing hers with her free hand, C.C. gave a half laugh. "We make a lousy team."

"It certainly looks that way." With his eyes on hers, Trent blew softly on her knuckles. Something flickered in those pretty green irises, he noted. Alarm, surprise, pleasure, he couldn't be sure, but he would have wagered half his stock options that C. C. Calhoun was totally ignorant of her aunt's romantic plotting.

He brought her hand to his lips—just a test, he assured himself—and watched what was definitely confusion darken her eyes. Her hand went limp in his. Her mouth opened and stayed that way, with no sound coming out.

"A kiss is supposed to make it better," he pointed out and, for purely selfish reasons, whispered his lips over her hand again.

"I think...it would be better if..." Lord, the room was small, she thought distractedly. And getting smaller all the time. "Thanks," she managed. "I'm sure it's fine now."

"It needs to be bandaged."

"Oh, well, I don't—"

"You'll only get it dirty." Enjoying himself enormously, he took a roll of gauze and began to wrap her hand.

Thinking it would put some distance between them, C.C. turned. As if following the moves of a dance, Trent turned as well. Now they were facing, rather than side-by-side. He shifted—there was room to do little else—and her back was against the wall.

"Hurt?"

She shook her head. She wasn't hurt, C.C. decided, she was crazy. A woman had to be crazy to have her heart pounding like a jackhammer because a man was wrapping gauze around her skinned knuckles.

"C.C." He taped the gauze competently in place. "Can I ask you a personal question?"

"I..." She lifted her shoulders and swallowed.

"What exactly is a lube job?"

She caught the amusement in his eyes, and, charmed by it, smiled back. "Forty-seven-fifty."

"Oh." They were as close as they had been the night before, when they'd been arguing. This, Trent decided, was much more pleasant. "Are you going to flush my radiator?"

"Absolutely."

"Then I'm forgiven for last night?"

Her brows lifted. "I didn't say that."

"I wish you'd reconsider." With her hand held between them, he shifted slightly closer. "You see, if I'm going to be damned for it, it's harder to resist the urge to sin again."

Flustered, she pressed back against the wall. "I don't think you're the least bit sorry about what you did."

He considered her a moment, the wide eyes, the tempting mouth. "I'm afraid you're right."

As she stood, torn between delight and terror, the phone began to shrill. "I've got to get that." Nimble as a greyhound, she streaked by him and out of the room.

He followed more slowly, surprised at himself. There was no doubt in his mind that she was as much victim of her aunt's fantasies as he. Another woman, certainly one with matrimony on her mind, would have smiled—or pouted. Would have slid her arms seductively around him—or held him sulkily away. But another woman would not have stood with her back planted against the wall as if facing a firing squad. Another woman would not have looked at him with big, helpless eyes and stammered.

Or looked so alluring while she did so.

C.C. snatched up the phone in her office, but her mind was blank. She stood, staring through the glass wall with the phone at her ear for ten silent seconds before the voice through the receiver brought her back.

"What? Oh, yes, yes, this is C.C. Sorry. Is that you, Finney?" She let out a long, pent-up breath as she listened. "Did you leave the lights on again? Are you sure? Okay, okay. It might be the starter motor." She ran a distracted hand through her hair and started to ease a hip down on the desk when she spotted Trent. She popped back up like a spring. "What? I'm sorry, could you say that again? Uh-huh. Why don't I come take a look at it on my way home? About six-thirty." Her lips curved. "Sure. I always have a taste for lobster. You bet. Bye."

"A mechanic who makes house calls," Trent commented.

"We take care of our own." Relax, she ordered herself. Relax right now. "Besides it's easy when there's the offer of an Albert Finney lob-stah dinner on the other end."

There was a tug of annoyance he tried mightily to ignore. "How's the hand?"

She wriggled her fingers. "Fine. Why don't you hang your keys on the pegboard?"

He did so. "Do you realize you've never called me by name?"

"Of course I have."

"No, you've called me names, but never by my name." He lifted a hand to gesture the thought away. "In any case, I need to talk to you."

"Listen, if it's about the house, this really isn't the time or place."

"It isn't, precisely."

"Oh." She looked at him, feeling that odd little jolt in her heart. "I'm really getting backed up. Can it wait until you pick up your car?"

He wasn't used to waiting for anything. "It won't take long. I feel I should warn you, as I believe you're as unaware as I was, of your aunt's plans."

"Aunt Coco? What plans?"

"The white-lace-and-orange-blossom type of plans."

Her expression went from baffled to stunned to suspicion. "Marriage? That's absurd. Aunt Coco's not planning to be married. She doesn't even see anyone seriously."

"I don't think she's the candidate." He walked toward her, keeping his eyes on her. "You are."

Her laugh was quick and full of fun as she sat on the edge of the desk. "Me? Married? That's rich."

"Yes, and so am I.'

Her laughter dried up. Using the palms of her hands, she levered herself off the desk. When she spoke, her voice was very cool, with licks of temper beneath. "Exactly what are you implying?"

"That your aunt, for reasons of her own, invited me here not only to look over the house, but her four very attractive nieces."

Her face went dead pale, as he now knew it did when she was desperately angry. "That's insulting."

"That's a fact."

"Get out." She gave him one hard shove toward the door. "Get out. Get your keys, your car and your ridiculous accusations and get out."

"Hold on and shut up for one minute." He took her firmly by the shoulders. "Just one minute, and when I'm done if you still think I'm being ridiculous, I'll leave."

"I know you're ridiculous. And conceited, and arrogant. If you think for one minute that I have—have designs on you—"

"Not you," he corrected with a little shake. "Your well-meaning aunt. 'Why don't you show Trenton the garden, C.C.? The flowers are exquisite in the moonlight.'"

"She was just being polite."

"In a pig's eye. Do you know how I spent my morning?"

"I couldn't be less interested."

"Looking through photo albums." He saw the anger turn to distress and pressed on. "Dozens of them. You were quite the adorable child, Catherine."

"Oh, God."

"And bright, too, according to your doting aunt. Spelling bee champ in the third grade."

With a strangled groan, she lowered to the desk again.

"Not a single cavity in your mouth."

"She didn't," C.C. managed.

"Oh, that and more. Top honors in your auto mechanics class in high school. Using the bulk of your inheritance to buy this shop from your employer. I'm told you're a very sensible woman who knows how to keep her feet on the ground. Then again, you come from excellent stock and were well-bred."

"Like a holstein," she muttered, firing up.

"As you like. Naturally, with your background, brains and beauty, you'd make the right man the most excellent of wives."

She was no longer pale, but blushing furiously. "Just because Aunt Coco's proud of me doesn't mean she's asking you to pick out a silver pattern."

"After she finished relating your virtues and showing me the pictures—quite lovely ones—of you in your prom dress."

"My—" C.C. only shut her eyes.

"She began to ask me my views on marriage and children. Dropping rather large, heavy hints that a man in my position needs a stable relationship with a stable woman. Such as yourself."

"All right, all right. Enough." She opened her eyes again. "Aunt Coco often gets ideas in her head about what's best for my sisters and me. If she goes overboard." C.C. set her teeth. "When she goes overboard, it's only because she loves us and feels responsible. I'm sorry she made you uncomfortable."

"I didn't tell you this to embarrass you or to have you apologize." Suddenly awkward, he slipped his hands into his pockets. "I thought it best if you knew the way her thoughts were headed before, well, something got out of hand."

"Got out of hand?" C.C. repeated.

"Or was misunderstood." Odd, he thought, it was usually so easy to lay the ground rules. He certainly couldn't remember fumbling before. "That is, after last night . . . I realize you've been sheltered to a certain degree."

The fingers of C.C.'s good hand began to drum on the knee of her coveralls.

Perhaps he should start again. "I believe in honesty, C.C., in both my business and my personal relationships. Last night, between temper and the moonlight, we—I suppose you could say we lost control for a moment." Why did that seem so pale and inadequate a description for what had happened? "I wouldn't want your lack of experience, and your aunt's fantasies to result in a misunderstanding."

"Let me see if I get this. You're concerned that because you kissed me last night, and my aunt brought up the subject of marriage along with my baby pictures this morning, that I might get some wild idea in my head that I might be the next Mrs. St. James."

Thrown off, he ran a hand over his hair. "More or less. I thought it would be better, certainly more fair, if I told you straight off so that you and I could handle it reasonably. That way you wouldn't—"

"Develop any delusions of grandeur?" she suggested.

"Don't put words in my mouth."

"How can I? There's no room with your foot in there."

"Damn it." He hated the fact that she was absolutely right. "I'm simply trying to be perfectly honest with you so that there won't be any misunderstanding when I tell you I'm very attracted to you."

She only lifted a brow, too furious to see that his own words had left him speechless. "Now, I take it, I'm supposed to be flattered."

"You're not supposed to be anything. I'm merely trying to lay out the facts."

"I'll give you some facts." She shoved a hand into his chest. "You're not attracted to me, you're attracted to the image of the perfect and enviable Trenton St. James III. My aunt's fantasies, as you call them, are a result of a wonderful loving heart. Something I'm sure you can't understand. And as far as I'm concerned, I wouldn't think about spending five minutes with you much less the rest of my life. You may end up with my home, but not with me, buster." She was revving up and feeling wonderful. "If you came crawling to me on your hands and knees with a diamond as big as my fist in your teeth, I'd laugh in your face. Those are the facts. I'm sure you can find your way out."

She turned and strode down the hall. Trent winced as the door slammed.

"Well," he murmured, pressing his fingers to his eyes. "We certainly cleared that up."

Chapter Five

Insufferable. It was the perfect word to describe him, C.C. decided, and hugged it to her throughout the rest of the day.

By the time she got home, the house was quiet and settled for the night. She could hear, faintly, the soft and haunting notes of the piano from the music room. Turning away from the stairs, she followed the music.

It was Suzanna, of course, who sat at the lovely old spinet. She had been the only one who had stuck with the lessons or shown any real talent. Amanda had been too impatient, Lilah too lazy. And C.C.... She looked down at her hands. Her fingers had been more at home smeared with motor oil than at the keys of a piano.

Still she loved to listen. There was nothing that soothed or charmed her more than music.

Suzanna, lost somewhere in her own heart, sighed a little as the last notes died.

"That was beautiful." C.C. walked over to kiss her sister's hair.

"I'm rusty."

"Not from where I'm standing."

Smiling, Suzanna reached back to pat her hand and felt the gauze. "Oh, C.C., what did you do?"

"Just scraped my knuckles."

"Did you clean it well? When was your last tetanus shot?"

"Slow down, Mommy. It's clean as a whistle and I had a tetanus shot six months ago." C.C. sat on the bench, facing out into the room. "Where is everyone?"

"The kids are fast asleep—I hope. Wiggle your fingers."

C.C. sighed and complied.

With a satisfied nod, Suzanna continued. "Lilah's out on a date. Mandy's looking over some ledger or other. Aunt Coco went up hours ago to have a bubble bath and put cucumber slices on her eyes."

"What about him?"

"In bed, I imagine. It's nearly midnight."

"Is it?" Then she smiled. "You were waiting up for me."

"I was not." Caught, Suzanna laughed. "Exactly. Did you fix Mr. Finney's truck?"

"He left his lights on again." She yawned hugely. "I think he does it on purpose just so I can come over and recharge his battery." She stretched her arms to the ceiling. "We had lobster and dandelion wine."

"If he wasn't old enough to be your grandfather, I'd say he has a crush on you."

"He does. And it's mutual. So, did I miss anything around here?"

"Aunt Coco wants to have a séance."

"Not again."

Suzanna ran her hands lightly over the keys, improvising. "Tomorrow night, right after dinner. She insists there's something Great-Grandmother Bianca wants us to know—Trent, too."

"What does he have to do with it?"

Suzanna brushed at C.C.'s bangs. "If we decide to sell him the house, he'll more or less inherit her."

"Is that what we're going to do, Suzanna?"

"It might be what we have to do."

C.C. rose to toy with the tassels of the floor lamp. "My business is doing pretty good. I could take out a loan against it."

"No."

"But—"

"No," Suzanna repeated. "You're not going to risk your future on the past."

"It's my future."

"And it's our past." She rose, as well. When that light came into Suzanna's eyes, even C.C. knew better than to argue. "I know how much the house means to you, to all of us. Coming back here after Bax—after things didn't work out," Suzanna said carefully, "helped keep me sane. Every time I watch Alex or Jenny slide down the banister, I remember doing it myself. I see Mama sitting here at the piano, hear Papa telling stories in front of the fire."

"Then how can you even think of selling?"

"Because I learned to face realities, however unpleasant." She lifted a hand to C.C.'s cheek. Only five years separated them. Sometimes Suzanna felt it was fifty. "Sometimes things happen to you, or around you, that you just can't control. When that happens, you gather up what's important in your life, and go on."

"But the house is important."

"How much longer do you really think we can hang on?"

"We could sell the lithographs, the Limoges, a few other things."

"And drag out the unhappiness." She knew entirely too much about that. "If it's time to let go, I think we should let go with some dignity."

"Then you've already made up your mind."

"No." Suzanna sighed and sat again. "Every time I think I have, I change it. Before dinner, the children and I walked along the cliffs." Eyes dreamy, she stared through the darkened window. "When I stand there, looking out over the bay, I feel something, something so incredible, it breaks my heart. I don't know what's right, C.C. I don't know what's best. But I'm afraid I know what has to be done."

"It hurts."

"I know."

C.C. sat beside her, rested her head on Suzanna's shoulder. "Maybe there'll be a miracle."

Trent watched them from the darkened hallway. He wished he hadn't heard them. He wished he didn't care. But he had heard, and for reasons he didn't choose to explore, he did care. Quietly he went back up the stairs.

* * *

"Children," Coco said with what she was certain was the last of her sanity, "why don't you read a nice book?"

"I want to play war." Alex swished an imaginary saber through the air. "Death to the last man."

And the child was only six, Coco thought. What would he be in ten years' time? "Crayons," she said hopefully, cursing rainy Saturday afternoons. "Why don't you both draw beautiful pictures? We can hang them on the refrigerator, like an art show."

"Baby stuff," Jenny said, a cynic at five. She hefted an invisible laser rifle and fired. "Z-z-zap! You're zapped, Alex, and totally disengrated."

"Disintergrated, dummy, and I am not either. I threw up my force field."

"Nuh-uh."

They eyed each other with the mutual dislike only siblings can feel after being cooped up on a Saturday. By tacit agreement, they switched to hand-to-hand combat. As they wrestled over the faded Aubusson carpet, Coco cast her gaze to the ceiling.

At least the match was taking place in Alex's room, so little harm could be done. She was tempted to go out and close the door, leaving them to finish up themselves, but she was, after all, responsible.

"Someone's going to get hurt," she began, in the age-old refrain of adult to child. "Remember what happened last week when Jenny gave you a bloody nose, Alex?"

"She did not." Masculine pride rose to the forefront as he struggled to pin his agile sister to the mat.

"Did too, did too," she chanted, hoping to do so again. She scissored her quick little legs over him.

"Excuse me," Trent said from the doorway. "I seem to be interrupting."

"Not at all." Coco fluffed her hair. "Just some youthful high spirits. Children, say hello to Mr. St. James."

"'Lo," Alex said as he struggled to get his sister into a headlock.

Trent's answering grin struck Coco with inspiration. "Trenton, might I ask you a favor?"

"Of course."

"All the girls are working today, as you know, and I have just one or two quick, little errands to run. Would you mind terribly keeping an eye on the children for a short time?"

"An eye on them?"

"Oh, they're no trouble at all." She beamed at him, then down at her grandniece and grandnephew. "Jenny, don't bite your brother. Calhouns fight fair." Unless they fight dirty, she thought. "I'll be back before you know I'm gone," she promised, easing past him.

"Coco, I'm not sure that I—"

"Oh, and don't forget about the séance tonight." She hurried down the steps and left him to fend for himself.

Jenny and Alex stopped wrestling to stare owlishly at him. They would fight tooth and nail but would unite without hesitation against an outside force.

"We don't like baby-sitters," Alex told him dangerously.

Trent rocked back on his heels. "I'm already sure I don't like being one."

Alex's arm was around his sister's shoulders now, rather than her neck. Hers slipped round his waist. "We don't like it more."

Trent nodded. If he could handle a staff of fifty, he could certainly handle two sulky children. "Okay."

"When we went back to Boston last summer for a visit, we had a sitter." Jenny eyed him with suspicion. "We made everybody's life a living hell."

Trent turned the chuckle into a cough. "Is that so?"

"Our father said we did," Alex corroborated. "And he was glad to see the back of us."

The infant profanity was no longer amusing. Trent struggled to keep the burn of anger out of his eyes and merely nodded. Baxter Dumont was obviously a prince among men. "I once locked my nanny in the closet and climbed out the window."

Alex and Jenny exchanged interested glances. "That's pretty good," Alex decided.

"She screamed for two hours," Trent improvised.

"We put a snake in our baby-sitter's bed and she ran out of the house in her nightgown." Jenny smiled smugly and waited to see if he could top it.

"Nicely done." What now? he wondered. "Have you any dolls?"

"Dolls are gross," Jenny said, loyal to her brother.

"Off with their heads!" Alex shouted, sending her into giggles. He sprang up, flourishing his imaginary sword. "I'm the evil pirate, and you're my prisoners."

"Uh-uh, I had to be prisoner last time." Jenny scrambled to her feet. "It's my turn to be the evil pirate."

"I said it first."

She gave him a hefty shove. "Cheater, cheater, cheater."

"Baby, baby, baby," he jeered, and pushed her back.

"Hold it!" Trent shouted before they could dive for each other. The unfamiliar masculine tone had them stopping in their tracks. "*I'm* the evil pirate," he told them, "and you're both about to walk the plank."

He enjoyed it. Their children's imagination might have been a bit bloody-minded, but they played fair when the rules were set. There would have been any number of people he knew socially who would have been stunned to see Trenton St. James III crawling around on the floor or firing a water pistol, but he could remember being closed in on rainy days himself.

The play went from pirates to space marauders to Indian rampage. At the end of a particularly gruesome battle, the three of them were sprawled on the floor. Alex, rubber tomahawk in hand, played dead so long he fell asleep.

"I won," Jenny said, then with her feather headdress falling over her eyes, cuddled against Trent's side. She, too, in the enviable way of children, was asleep in moments.

C.C. found them like that. The rain was patting gently at the windows. In the bath down the hall, a drip fell musically into a bucket. Otherwise there was only the sound of gentle, even breathing.

Alex was sprawled on his face, his fingers still clutched over his weapon. In addition to bodies, the floor was scattered with miniature cars, defeated action figures and a few plastic dinosaurs. Avoiding the casualties, she stepped inside.

She wasn't exactly sure what her feelings were at finding Trent sleeping on the floor with her niece and nephew. What she was certain of was that if she hadn't seen it for herself, she wouldn't have believed it.

His tie and shoes were gone, his hair mussed, and there was a streak of damp down his linen shirt.

The tug on her heart was slow and tender and very real. Why, he looked...sweet, she thought, then immediately jammed her hands into her pockets. That was absurd. A man like Trent was never sweet.

Maybe the kids had knocked him unconscious, she mused, and leaned over him. He opened his eyes, stared up at her for a moment, then made some kind of sleepy noise deep in his throat.

"What are you doing?" she whispered.

"I'm not completely sure." He lifted his head and looked around. Jenny was tucked into the curve of his arm, and Alex was down for the count on the other side. "But I think I'm the only survivor."

"Where's Aunt Coco?"

"Running a few errands. I'm keeping my eye on the kids."

She lifted a brow. "Oh, I can see that."

"I'm afraid there was a major battle, and many lives were lost."

C.C.'s lips twitched as she went to Alex's bed for a blanket. "Who won?"

"Jenny claimed victory." Gently he slipped his arm out from under her head. "Though Alex will disagree."

"Undoubtedly."

"What should we do with them?"

"Oh, we'll keep them, I suppose."

He grinned back at her. "No, I meant should they be put in bed or something?"

"No." Expertly she flipped open the blanket and spread it over both of them where they lay. "They'll be fine." She had a ridiculous urge to slip an arm around his waist and lay her head on his shoulder. She squashed it ruthlessly. "It was nice of you to offer to look after them."

"I didn't offer precisely. I was dragooned."

"It was still nice of you."

He caught up with her at the door. "I could use a cup of coffee."

C.C. hesitated only a moment. "All right. I'll fix it. It looks like you've earned it." She flicked a glance over her shoulder as she started down the stairs. "How'd your shirt get wet?"

"Oh." He brushed a hand over it, faintly embarrassed. "A direct hit with a death ray disguised as a water pistol. So, how was your day?"

"Not nearly as adventurous as yours." She turned into the kitchen and went directly to the stove. "I only rebuilt an engine."

When the coffee was started, she moved over to light a fire in the kitchen hearth. She had rain in her hair, Trent noticed. He wasn't a lyrical man, but he found himself thinking that the droplets of water looked like a shower of diamonds against the glossy cap.

He'd always preferred women with long hair, he reminded himself. Feminine, soft, wavy. And yet...the style suited C.C., showing off her slender neck, perfectly framing that glorious white skin.

"What are you staring at?"

He blinked, shook his head. "Nothing. Sorry, I was just thinking. It's ah . . . there's something comforting about a fire in the kitchen."

"Hmm." He looked weird, she thought. Maybe it was the lack of a tie. "Do you want milk in your coffee?"

"No, black."

Her arm brushed his as she walked to the stove. This time it was he who stepped back. "Did Aunt Coco say where she was going?"

Maybe there was static electricity in the air, he thought. That would explain the jolt he'd felt when he'd touched her. "Not exactly. It doesn't matter, the kids were entertaining."

She studied his face as she handed him a mug. "I think you mean it."

"I do. Maybe I haven't been around children enough to become jaded. Those two are quite a pair."

"Suzanna's a terrific mother." Comfortable, she leaned back against the counter as she sipped. "She used to practice on me. So, how's the car running?"

"Better than it has in months." He toasted her with the mug. "I'm afraid I didn't notice anything was off until after you'd worked on it. I don't really know anything about engines."

"That's all right. I don't know how to plot a corporate takeover."

"I was sorry you weren't there when I came around to pick it up. Hank said you'd gone to dinner. I guess you had a good time—you didn't get in until late."

"I always have a good time with Finney." She turned around to raid the cookie jar, then offered him one as he tried to ignore the little nip of jealousy.

"An old friend?"

"I guess you could say so." C.C. took a deep breath and prepared to launch into the speech she had practiced all day. "I'd like to straighten out the business you brought up yesterday."

"It isn't necessary. I got the picture."

"I could have explained things without being so hard on you."

He tilted his head, studying her thoughtfully. "You could have?"

"I like to think so." Determined to wipe the slate clean, she set the coffee aside. "I was embarrassed, and being embarrassed makes me angry. This whole situation is difficult."

He could still hear, very clearly, the unhappiness in her voice as she had spoken with Suzanna the night before. "I think I'm beginning to understand that."

Her eyes came back to his, and she sighed. "Well, in any case, I can't help but resent the fact that you want to buy The Towers, or that we might have to let you—but that's a separate thing from Aunt Coco's maneuvers. I think I realized, after I stopped being mad, that you were just as embarrassed as I was. You were just so damned polite."

"It's a bad habit of mine."

"You're telling me." She waved half a cookie at him. "If you hadn't brought up the kiss—"

"I understand that was an error in judgment, but since I'd already apologized for it, I thought we could deal with it reasonably."

"I didn't want an apology," C.C. muttered. "Then or now."

"I see."

"No, you don't. You certainly don't. What I meant was that an apology was unnecessary. I may be inexperienced by your standards, and I may not be sophisticated like the women you're used to dealing with, but I'm not foolish enough to start weaving daydreams out of one stupid kiss." She was getting angry again and was determined not to. After one deep, cleansing breath, she tried again. "I'd simply like to put that, and our conversation yesterday behind us, completely and totally. If it turns out that we will have business dealings, it would be wiser all around if we can be civilized."

"I like you this way."

"What way?"

"When you're not taking potshots at me."

She finished off her cookie and grinned. "Don't get used to it. All Calhouns have hideous tempers."

"So I've been warned. Truce?"

"I suppose. Want another cookie?"

He was staring again, she noted, and her own eyes widened when he reached out to brush his fingertips down her hair. "What are you doing?"

"Your hair's wet." He stroked it again, fascinated. "It smells like wet flowers."

"Trent—"

He smiled. "Yes?"

"I don't think this is the best way to handle things."

"Probably not." But his fingers trailed down through her hair to the nape of her neck. He felt her quick shudder. "I can't quite get you out of my mind.

And I keep having these uncontrollable urges to get my hands on you. I wonder why.''

"Because—" she wet her lips "—I irritate you."

"Oh, you do that, without question." He pressed those fingers at the back of her neck and had her moving forward an inch. "But not simply in the way you mean. It's not simple at all. Though it should be." His other hand skimmed over the collar of her denim work shirt, then cupped her chin. "Otherwise, why would I feel this irresistible need to touch you every time I get near you?"

"I don't know." His fingers, light as a feather, trailed down to where her pulse thudded at the base of her throat. "I wish you wouldn't."

"Wouldn't what?"

"Touch me."

He slid his hand down her sleeve to her bandaged hand, then lifted it to his lips. "Why?"

"Because you make me nervous."

Something lit in his eyes, turning them almost black. "You don't even mean to be provocative, do you?"

"I wouldn't know how." Her eyes fluttered closed on a strangled moan when he brushed his lips over her jawline.

"Honeysuckle," he murmured, drawing her closer. He'd once thought it such a common flower. "I can all but taste it on you. Wild and sweet."

Her muscles turned to water as his mouth cruised over hers. So much lighter, so much gentler than the first time. It wasn't right that he could do this to her. The part of her mind that was still rational all but shouted it. But even that was drowned out by the flood of longing.

"Catherine." He had her face framed between his hands now as he nipped seductively at her lips. "Kiss me back."

She wanted to shake her head, to pull away and walk casually, even callously out of the room. Instead she flowed into his arms, her mouth lifting to his, meeting his.

His fingers tightened before he could prevent it, then slipped down to pull her more truly against him. He could think of nothing, wanted to think of nothing—no consequences, no rules, no code of behavior. For the first time in his memory, he wanted only to feel. Those sharp and sweet sensations she had racing through him were more than enough for any man.

She was strong—had always been strong—but not enough to prevent time from standing still. It was this one moment, she realized, that she had been waiting for all of her life. As her hands slid up his back, she held the moment to her as completely as she held him.

The fire crackled in the grate. The rain pattered. There was the light, spicy scent of the potpourri Lilah set everywhere about the house. His arms were so strong and sure, yet with a gentleness she hadn't expected from him.

She would remember it all, every small detail, along with the dark excitement of his mouth and the sound of her name as he whispered it against hers.

He drew her away, slowly this time, more shaken than he cared to admit. As he watched, she ran her tongue over her lips as if to savor a last taste. That small, unconscious gesture nearly brought him to his knees.

"No apology this time," he told her, and his voice wasn't steady.

"No."

He touched his lips to hers again. "I want you. I want to make love with you."

"Yes." It was a glorious kind of release. Her lips curved against his. "Yes."

"When?" He buried his face in her hair. "Where?"

"I don't know." She shut her eyes on the wonder of it. "I can't think."

"Don't." He kissed her temple, her cheekbone, her mouth. "This isn't the time for thinking."

"It has to be perfect."

"It will be." He framed her face again. "Let me show you."

She believed him—the words and what she saw in his eyes. "I can't believe it's going to be you." Laughing, she threw her arms around him, holding him close. "That I've waited all my life to be with someone. And it's you."

His hand paused on its way to her hair. "All of your life?"

Dreamily in love, she hugged him tighter. "I thought I'd be afraid the first time, but I'm not. Not with you."

"The first time." He shut his eyes. *Her* first time. How could he have been so stupid? He'd recognized the inexperience, but he hadn't thought, hadn't believed she was completely innocent. And he'd all but seduced her in her own kitchen. "C.C."

"I'm thirsty," Alex complained from the doorway, and had them springing apart like guilty children. He eyed them suspiciously. "What are you doing that stuff for? It's disgusting." He sent Trent a pained look, man-to-man. "I don't get why anybody wants to go around kissing girls."

"It's an acquired taste," Trent told him. "Why don't we get you a drink, then I need to talk to your aunt a minute. Privately."

"More mush stuff."

"What mush stuff?" Amanda wanted to know as she breezed in.

"Nothing." C.C. reached for the coffeepot.

"Lord, did I have a day," Amanda began, and grabbed a cookie.

Suzanna walked in two seconds later, followed by Lilah. As the kitchen filled with feminine laughter and scent, Trent knew his moment was lost.

When C.C. smiled at him across the room, he was afraid his head would be lost with it.

Chapter Six

It was Trent's first séance. He sincerely hoped it would be his last. There was simply no gracious way to decline attending. When he suggested that perhaps this was a family evening, Coco merely laughed and patted his cheek.

"My dear, we wouldn't think of excluding you. Who knows, it may be you the restless spirits choose to speak through."

The possibility did very little to cheer him up.

Once the children were tucked into bed for the evening, the rest of the family, along with the reluctant Trent, gathered around the dining room table. The stage had been set.

A dozen candles flickered atop the buffet. Dime-store holders cheek by jowl with Meissen and Baccarat. Another trio of white tapers glowed in the center of the table. Even nature seemed to have gotten into the spirit of things—so to speak.

Outside, the rain had turned into a wet fitful snow, blown about by a rising wind. As warm and cold air collided, thunder boomed and lightning flickered.

It was a dark and stormy night, Trent thought fatalistically as he took his seat.

Coco had not, as he'd secretly feared, worn a turban and a fringed shawl. As always, she was meticulously groomed. Around her neck, she did wear a large amethyst crystal, which she toyed with constantly.

"Now, children," she instructed. "Take hands and form the circle."

The wind knocked at the windows as C.C. slipped her hand into Trent's. Coco took his other. Directly across from him Amanda grinned, the amusement and sympathy obvious as she linked with her aunt and Suzanna.

"Don't worry, Trent," she told him. "The Calhoun ghosts are always well behaved around company."

"Concentration is essential," Lilah explained as she closed the gap between her eldest and youngest sister. "And very basic, really. All you have to do is clear your mind, particularly of any cynicism." She winked at Trent. "Astrologically, it's an excellent night for a séance."

C.C. gave his hand a quick, reassuring squeeze as Coco took over.

"We must all clear our minds and open our hearts." She spoke in a soothing monotone. "For some time I've felt that my grandmother, the unhappy Bianca, has wanted to contact me. This was her summer home for the last years of her young life. The place where she spent her most joyous and most tragic moments. The place where she met the man she loved, and lost.''

She closed her eyes and took a deep breath. ''We are here, Grandmama, waiting for you. We know your spirit is troubled.''

''Does a spirit have a spirit?'' Amanda wanted to know and earned a glare from her aunt. ''It's a reasonable question.''

''Behave,'' Suzanna murmured, and smothered a smile. ''Go ahead, Aunt Coco.''

They sat in silence, with only Coco's voice murmuring over the crackle of the fire and the moan of the wind. Trent's mind wasn't clear. It was filled with the way C.C. had fit in his arms, with the sweet and generous way her mouth had opened to his. The way she had looked at him, her eyes clouded and warm with emotions. Emotions he had recklessly stirred in her.

Guilt almost smothered him.

She wasn't like Marla or any of the women he had coolly romanced over the years. She was innocent and open and, despite a strong will and a sharp tongue, achingly vulnerable. He had taken advantage of that, inexcusably.

Not that it was entirely his fault, he reminded himself. She was, after all, a beautiful, desirable woman. And he was human. The fact that he wanted her— strictly on a physical plane—was only natural.

He glanced over just as she turned her head and smiled at him. Trent had to fight down a foolish urge to lift her hand to his lips and taste her skin.

She touched something in him, damn it. Something he was determined would remain untouched.

When she smiled at him—even when she scowled at him—she made him feel more, want more, wish more, than any woman he'd ever known.

It was ridiculous. They were miles apart in every way. And yet, with her hand warm in his as it was now, he felt closer to her, more in tune with her, than he'd ever felt with anyone.

He could even see them sitting together on a sunny summer porch, watching children play on the grass. The sound of the sea was as soothing as a lullaby. The air smelled of roses climbing up the trellis. And of honeysuckle, growing wild where it chose.

He blinked, afraid his heart had stopped. The image had been so clear and so terrifying. It was the atmosphere, he assured himself. The candles flickering, the wind and lightning. It was playing games with his imagination.

He wasn't a man to sit on the porch with a woman and watch children. He had work, a business to run. The idea of him becoming involved with a bad-tempered auto mechanic was simply absurd.

Cold air seemed to slap him in the face. As he stiffened, he saw the flames of the candles lean dramatically to the left. A draft, he told himself, as the cold chilled him to the bone. The place was full of them.

He felt C.C.'s shudder. When he looked at her, her eyes were wide and dark. Her fingers curled tight around his.

"She's here!" There was both surprise and excitement in Coco's voice. "I'm sure of it."

In her delight, she nearly pulled her hands free and broke the chain. She had believed—well, had wanted to believe—but she had never actually felt a *presence* so distinctly.

She beamed down the table at Lilah, but her niece had her eyes closed and a faint smile on her lips.

"A window must have come open," Amanda said, and would have bolted up to check if Coco hadn't hissed at her.

"No such thing. Sit still, everyone. Sit still. She's here. Can't you feel it?"

C.C. did, and wasn't sure whether she should feel foolish or frightened. Something was different. She was certain that Trent sensed it, as well.

It was as though someone had gently closed a hand over her and Trent's joined ones. The cold vanished, replaced by a soothing, comforting warmth. So real was it that C.C. looked over her shoulder, certain she would see someone standing behind her.

Yet all she saw was the dance of fire and candle-light on the wall.

"She's so lost." C.C. let out a gasp when she realized it was she herself who had spoken. All eyes fixed on hers. Even Lilah's lazily opened.

"Do you see her?" Coco demanded in a whisper, squeezing C.C.'s fingers.

"No. No, of course not. It's just..." She couldn't explain. "It's so sad," she murmured, unaware that tears glistened in her eyes. "Can't you feel it?"

Trent could, and it left him speechless. Heart-break, and a longing so deep it was immeasurable. Imagination, he told himself. The power of sugges-tion.

"Don't close it off." Coco searched desperately for the proper procedure. Now that something had actually happened, she hadn't a clue. A flash of lightning had her jolting. "Do you think she'll speak through you?"

At the opposite end of the table, Lilah smiled. "Just tell us what you see, honey."

"A necklace," C.C. heard herself say. "Two tiers of emeralds flanked by diamonds. Beautiful, brilliant." The gleam hurt her eyes. "She's wearing them, but I can't see her face. Oh, she's so unhappy."

"The Calhoun necklace," Coco breathed. "So, it's true."

Then, as if a sigh passed through the air, the candles flickered again, then ran straight and true. A log fell in the grate.

"Weird," Amanda said when her aunt's hand fell limply from hers. "I'll fix the fire."

"Honey." Suzanna studied C.C. with as much concern as curiosity. "Are you okay?"

"Yes." C.C. cleared her throat. "Sure." She shot Trent a quick look. "I guess the storm got to me."

Coco lifted a hand to her breast and patted her speeding heart. "I think we could all use a nice glass of brandy." She rose, more shaken than she wanted to admit, and walked to the buffet.

"Aunt Coco," C.C. began. "What's the Calhoun necklace?"

"The emeralds." She passed the snifters. "There was a legend that's been handed down through the family. You know part of it, how Bianca fell in love with another man, and died tragically. I suppose it's time I told you the rest of it."

"You kept a secret?" Amanda grinned as she swirled her drink. "Aunt Coco, you amaze me."

"I wanted to wait for the right time. It seems it's now." She took her seat again, warming the brandy between her hands. "Rumor was that Bianca's lover was an artist, one of the many who came to the island in those days. She would go to meet him when Fergus was away from the house, which was often. Theirs was not precisely an arranged marriage, but the next thing to it. She was years younger than he, and apparently quite beautiful. Since Fergus destroyed all pictures of her after her death, there's no way of knowing for sure."

"Why?" Suzanna asked. "Why would he do that?"

"Grief perhaps." Coco shrugged.

"Rage, more likely," Lilah put in.

"In any case." Coco paused to sip. "He destroyed all reminders of her, and the emeralds were lost. He had given Bianca the necklace when she gave birth to Ethan, her eldest son." She glanced at Trent. "My father. He was just a child at the time of his mother's death, so the events were never very clear in his mind. But his nanny, who had been fiercely loyal to Bianca, would tell him stories about her. And those he remembered. She didn't care for the necklace, but wore it often."

"As a kind of punishment," Lilah put in. "And a kind of talisman." She smiled at her aunt. "Oh, I've known about the necklace for years. I've seen it—just as C.C. did tonight." She lifted the brandy to her lips. "There are earrings to match. Emerald teardrops, like the stone in the center of the bottom tier."

"You're making that up," Amanda accused her, and Lilah merely moved her shoulders.

"No, I'm not." She smiled at C.C. "Am I?"

"No." Uneasy, C.C. looked to her aunt. "What does all this mean?"

"I'm not altogether sure, but I think the necklace is still important to Bianca. It was never seen after she died. Some believed Fergus threw it into the sea."

"Not on your life," Lilah said. "The old man wouldn't have thrown a nickel into the sea, much less an emerald necklace."

"Well..." Coco didn't like to speak ill of an ancestor, but she was forced to agree. "Actually, it would have been out of character. Grandpapa counted his pennies."

"He made Silas Marner look like a philanthropist," Amanda put in. "So, what happened to it?"

"That, my dear, is the mystery. My father's nanny told him that Bianca was going to leave Fergus, that she had packed a box, what the nanny called a treasure box. Bianca had secreted away what was most valuable to her."

"But she died instead," C.C. murmured.

"Yes. The legend is that the box, with its treasure, is hidden somewhere in the house."

"Our house?" Suzanna gaped at her aunt. "Do you really think there's some kind of treasure chest hidden around here for—what—eighty years, and no one's found it?"

"It's a very big house," Coco pointed out. "For all we know she might have buried it in the roses."

"If it existed in the first place," Amanda murmured.

"It existed." Lilah sent a nod toward C.C. "And I think Bianca's decided it's time to find it."

When everyone began to talk at once, arguments and suggestions bouncing around the table, Trent raised a hand. "Ladies. Ladies," he repeated, waiting for them to subside. "I realize that this is family business, but as I was invited to participate in this... experiment, I feel obligated to add a calming note. Legends are most often exaggerated and expanded over time. If there ever was a necklace, wouldn't it be more likely that Fergus sold it after the death of his wife?"

"He couldn't sell it," Lilah pointed out, "if he couldn't find it."

"Do any of you really think your great-grandfather buried treasure in the garden or hid it behind a loose stone?" One glance around the table told him that was precisely how they were thinking. Trent shook his head. "That kind of fairy tale's more suited for Alex and Jenny than for grown women." He spread his hands. "You don't even know for certain if there was a necklace in the first place."

"But I saw it," C.C. said, though it made her feel foolish.

"You imagined it," he corrected. "Think about it. A few minutes ago six rational adults were sitting around this table holding hands and calling up ghosts. All right as an odd sort of parlor game, but for anyone to actually believe in messages from the otherworld..." He certainly wasn't going to add that for a moment, he'd felt something himself.

"There's something appealing about a cynical, practical-minded man." Lilah rose to open one of the drawers of the buffet and unearthed a pad and pencil. After coming over to kneel by C.C.'s chair, she began to sketch. "I certainly respect your opinion, but the fact is not only did the necklace exist, I'm certain it still does."

"Because of a nanny's bedtime stories?"

She smiled at him. "No, because of Bianca." She slid the pad toward C.C. "Is that what you saw tonight?"

Lilah had always been a careless and clever artist. C.C. stared at the rough sketch of the necklace, two ornate and filigreed tiers studded with square-cut emeralds, sprinkled with diamond brilliants. From the bottom tier a large gem in the shape of a teardrop dripped.

"Yes." C.C. traced a fingertip over it. "Yes, this is it."

Trent studied the drawing. If indeed such a piece did exist, and Lilah's drawing was anywhere close to scale, it would undoubtedly be worth a fortune.

"Oh, my," Coco murmured as the pad was passed to her. "Oh, my."

"I think Trent has a point." Amanda gave the sketch a hard look before handing it to Suzanna. "We can hardly take the house apart stone by stone, even if we wanted to. Despite any sort of paranormal experience, the first order of business is to make certain—absolutely certain," she added when Lilah sighed, "that the necklace is a fact. Even eighty years ago, something like this had to cost an incredible amount of money. There has to be a record. If Lilah's famous vibes are wrong and it was sold again, there would be a record of that as well."

"Spoken like a true stick-in-the-mud," Lilah complained. "I guess this means we spend our Sunday pushing through a paper mountain."

C.C. didn't even try to sleep. She wrapped herself in her flannel robe and, with the house creaking around her, left her room for Trent's. She could hear the murmur of the late news from Amanda's room. Then the hum of sitars from Lilah's. It didn't occur to her to feel awkward or to hesitate. She simply knocked on Trent's door and waited for him to answer.

When he did, with his shirt open and his eyes a little sleepy, she felt her first frisson of nerves.

"C.C.?"

"I need to talk to you." She glanced toward the bed, then away. "Can I come in?"

How was a man to deal fairly when even flannel had become erotic? "Maybe it would be better if we waited until morning."

"I'm not sure I can."

The knots in his stomach tightened. "Okay. Sure." The sooner he explained himself to her, the better. He hoped. Trent let her in and closed the door. "Do you want to sit down?"

"Too much nervous energy." Hugging herself, she walked to the window. "It stopped snowing. I'm glad. I know Suzanna was worried about some of her flowers. Spring's so unpredictable on the island." She dragged a hand through her hair as she turned. "I'm making small talk, and I hate that." A deep breath settled her. "Trent, I need to know what you think about tonight. Really think about it."

"Tonight?" he said carefully.

"The séance." She rubbed her hands over her face. "Lord, I feel like an imbecile even saying it, but, Trent, something happened." Now she thrust those restless hands toward him, waiting for him to clasp them in his. "I'm very grounded, very literal minded. Lilah's the one who believes in all this stuff. But now... Trent, I need to know. Did you feel anything?"

"I don't know what you mean. I certainly felt foolish several times."

"Please." She gave his hands an impatient shake. "Be honest with me. It's important."

Isn't that what he'd promised himself he would do? "All right, C.C. Tell me what you felt."

"The air got very cold. Then it was as if something—someone—was standing behind us. Behind and between the two of us. It wasn't something that frightened me. I was surprised, but not afraid. We were holding hands, like this. And then..."

She was waiting for him to say it, to admit it. Those big green eyes demanded it. When he did so, it was with great reluctance. "It felt as though someone put a hand over ours."

"Yes." Eyes closed, she brought his hands to her curved lips. "Yes, exactly."

"Shared hallucination," he began, but she cut him off with a laugh.

"I don't want to hear that. No rational explanations." She pressed his hand to her cheek. "I'm not a fanciful person, but I know it meant something, something important. I *know*."

"The necklace?"

"Only a part of it—and not this part. All the rest—
the necklace, the legend, we'll figure it out sooner or
later. I think we'll have to because it's meant. But this,
this was like a blessing."

"C.C.—"

"I love you." Eyes dark and brilliant, she touched
his cheek. "I love you, and nothing in my life has ever
felt so right."

He was speechless. Part of him wanted to step back,
smile kindly and tell her she was letting the moment
run away with her. Love didn't happen in a matter of
days. If it happened at all, which was rare, it took
years.

Another part, buried deep, wanted to hold her close
so that the moment would never end.

"Catherine—"

But she was already moving into his arms. They
seemed to be waiting for her. As if he had no control
over them, they wrapped around her. The warmth, her
warmth, seeped into him like a drug.

"I think I knew the first time you kissed me." She
pressed her cheek to his. "I didn't want it, didn't ask
for it, but it's never been like that for me before. I
don't think I ever expected it to be. There you were, so
suddenly, so completely in my life. Kiss me again,
Trent. Kiss me now."

He was helpless to do otherwise. His lips were already burning for hers. When they met, the fire only
sparked hotter. She was molten in his arms, sending
white licks of flame shooting through his system.
When he couldn't prevent his demand from increasing, she didn't hesitate, but strained against him, offering everything.

She slid her hands under his shirt, delighted to feel his quick, involuntary tremor. His muscles bunched under her fingers with the kind of strength she wanted, needed.

The wind sighed outside the windows as she sighed in his arms.

He couldn't get enough. He found himself wanting to devour her as his lips raced crazily over her face, down her throat where his teeth scraped lightly over her skin. The scent of honeysuckle wheeled in his head. She arched back, her low whimpers of pleasure pounding in his blood.

He had to touch her. He would go mad if he didn't. Mad if he did. When he parted her robe, he groaned, discovering she was naked for him beneath. Desperate, he filled his hand with her.

Now she knew what it was to have the blood swim. She could all but feel it racing under her skin, beating hot wherever he touched. There was a weakness here, a glorious one, mixed with a kind of manic strength. She wanted to give him both somehow and found the way when his mouth came frantically back to hers.

She trembled even as she answered. She surrendered even as she heated. As her head fell back and her fingers dug hard into his shoulders, he felt something move through him that was more than desire, deeper than passion.

Happiness. Hope. Love. As he recognized the feelings, terror joined them.

Breath heaving, he pulled away.

Her robe had fallen off one shoulder, baring it. Already his mouth had supped there. Her eyes were as brilliant as the emeralds she had imagined. Smiling, she lifted a trembling hand to his cheek.

"Do you want me to stay tonight?"

"Yes—no." Holding her at arm's length was the hardest thing he'd ever done. "Catherine..." He did want her to stay, he realized. Not just tonight, and not simply because of that glorious body of hers. The fact that he did made it all the more important to set things right. "I don't—I haven't been fair with you, and this has gotten out of hand so quickly." A long, unsteady breath escaped him. "Lord, you're beautiful. No," he said quickly when she smiled and started to step forward. "We need to talk. Just talk."

"I thought we had."

If she continued to look at him that way, he'd stop giving a damn about fairness. Or his own survival. "I haven't made myself clear," he began slowly. "If I had known—if I had realized how completely innocent you are, I wouldn't—well, I hope I would have been more careful. Now I can only try to make up for it."

"I don't understand."

"No, that's the problem." Needing some distance, he walked away. "I said I was attracted to you, very attracted. And that's obviously true. But I would never have taken advantage of you if I had known."

Suddenly cold, she drew the robe around her. "You're upset because I haven't been with a man before?"

"Not upset." Frustrated, he turned back. " 'Upset' isn't the word. I can't seem to find one. There are rules, you see." But she only continued to stare at him. "Catherine, a woman like you expects—deserves— more than I can give you."

She lowered her gaze to her hands as she carefully fastened the belt to her robe. "What is that?"

"Commitment. A future."

"Marriage."

"Yes."

Her knuckles were turning white. "I suppose you think this—what I said—is part of Aunt Coco's plans."

"No." He would have gone to her then if he'd dared. "No, of course I don't."

"Well." She struggled to make her fingers relax. "That's something, I suppose."

"I know your feelings are honest—exaggerated perhaps—but honest. And it's completely my fault. If this hadn't happened so quickly, I would have explained to you from the first that I have no intention of marrying, ever. I don't believe that two people can be loyal to each other, much less happy together for a lifetime."

"Why?"

"Why?" He stared at her. "Because it simply doesn't work. I've watched my father go from marriage to divorce to marriage. It's like watching a tennis match. The last time I heard from my mother, she was on her third marriage. It simply isn't practical to make vows knowing they'll only be broken."

"Practical," she repeated with a slow nod. "You won't let yourself feel anything for me because it would be impractical."

"The problem is I do feel something for you."

"Not enough." Only enough to cut out her heart. "Well, I'm glad we got that sorted out." Blindly she turned for the door. "Good night."

"C.C." He laid a hand on her shoulder before she could find the knob.

"Don't apologize," she said, praying her control would hold a few more minutes. "It isn't necessary. You've explained it all perfectly."

"Damn it, why don't you yell at me? Call me a few of the names I'm sure I deserve." He'd have preferred that to the quiet desolation he'd seen in her eyes.

"Yell at you?" She made herself turn and face him. "For being fair and honest? Call you names? How can I call you names, Trent, when I feel so terribly sorry for you?"

His hand slipped away from her. She held her head up. Under the hurt, just under it, was pride.

"You're throwing away something—no, not throwing," she corrected. "You're politely handing back something you'll never have again. What you've turned out of your life, Trent, would have been the best part of it."

She left him alone with the uneasy feeling that she was absolutely right.

There was a party tonight. I thought it would be good for me to fill the house with people and lights and flowers. I know that Fergus was pleased that I supervised all the details so carefully. I had wondered if he had noticed my distraction, or how often I walked along the cliffs these afternoons, or how many hours I have begun to spend in the tower, dreaming my dreams. But it does not seem so.

The Greenbaums were here, and the McAllisters and the Prentises. Everyone who summers on the island, that Fergus feels we should take note of, attended. The ballroom was banked with gardenias and red roses. Fergus had hired an orchestra from New York, and the music was both lovely and lively. I believe Sarah McAllister drank too much champagne, for her laugh began to grate on my nerves long before supper was served.

My new gold dress suited very well, I think, for it gathered many compliments. Yet when I danced with Ira Greenbaum, his eyes were on my emeralds. They hung like a shackle around my neck.

How unfair I am! They are beautiful, and mine only because Ethan is mine.

During the evening, I slipped up to the nursery to check on the children, though I know how doting Nanny is to all of them. Ethan woke and sleepily asked if I had brought him any cake.

He looks like an angel as he sleeps, he, and my other sweet babies. My love for them is so rich, so deep, that I wonder why it is my heart cannot transfer any of that sweet feeling to the man who fathered them.

Perhaps the fault is in me. Surely that must be so. When I kissed them good-night and stepped out into the hall again, I wished so desperately that rather than go back to the ballroom to laugh and dance, I could run to the cliffs. To stand at the cliffs with the wind in my hair and the sound and smells of the sea everywhere.

Would he come to me then, if I dared such a thing? Would he come so that we would stand there together in the shadows, reaching out for something we have no business wanting, much less taking?

I did not go to the cliffs. My duty is my husband, and it was to him I went. Dancing with him, my heart felt as cold as the jewels around my neck. Yet I smiled when he complimented me on my skill as a hostess. His hand at my waist was so aloof, but so possessive. As we moved to the music, his eyes scanned the room, approving what was his, studying his guests to be certain they were impressed.

How well I know what status and opinion mean to the man I married. And how little it seems they have come to mean to me.

I wanted to shout at him. "Fergus, for God's sake, look at me. Look at me and see. Make me love you, for fear and respect cannot be enough for either of us. Make me love you so that I will never again turn my steps toward the cliffs and what waits for me there."

But I did not shout. When he told me impatiently that it was necessary for me to dance with Cecil Barkley, I murmured my assent.

Now the music is done and the lamps are snuffed out. I wonder when I will see Christian again. I wonder what will become of me.

Chapter Seven

C.C. sat cross-legged in the center of an ocean of papers. Her assignment—whether or not she'd chosen to accept it—had been to go through all of the notes and receipts and scraps that had been stuffed into three cardboard boxes marked miscellaneous.

Nearby Amanda sat at a card table, with several more bulging boxes at her feet. With her hair clipped back and reading glasses sliding down her nose, she meticulously studied each paper before laying it on one of the various stacks she had started.

"This should have been done decades ago," she commented.

"You mean it should have been burned decades ago."

"No." Amanda shoved the glasses back into place. "Some of it's fascinating, and certainly deserves to be preserved. Stuffing papers into cardboard boxes is not my idea of preserving family history.''

"Does a recipe for gooseberry jam rate as family history?''

"For Aunt Coco it does. That goes under kitchen, subheading menus.''

C.C. shifted then waved away a cloud of dust. "How about a bill for six pair of white kid gloves and a blue silk parasol?''

"Clothing, by the date. Hmm, this is interesting. Aunt Coco's progress report from her fourth-grade teacher. And I quote, 'Cordelia is a delightfully gregarious child. However, she tends to daydream and has trouble finishing assigned projects.''

"That's a news flash.'' Stiff, C.C. arched her back and rotated her head. Beside her, the sun was streaming through the smudges on the storeroom window. With a little sigh, she rested her elbows on her knees and studied it.

"Where the devil is Lilah?'' Impatient as always, Amanda tapped her foot as she grumbled. "Suzanna had dispensation because she took the kids to the matinee, but Lilah's supposed to be on duty.''

"She'll show up,'' C.C. murmured.

"Sure. When it's done.'' Digging into a new pile, Amanda sneezed twice. "This is some of the dirtiest stuff I've ever seen.''

C.C. shrugged. "Everything gets dirty if it sits around long enough.''

"No, I mean really dirty. It's a limerick written by Great-Uncle Sean. 'There was a young lady from Maine, whose large breasts drove the natives insane. They...' Never mind,'' Amanda decided. "We'll start a file on attempted pornography." When C.C. made no comment, she glanced over to see her sister still staring at a sunbeam. "You okay, sweetie?"

"Hmm? Oh, yeah. I'm fine."

"You don't look like you slept very well."

C.C. shrugged then busied herself with papers again. "I guess the séance threw me off."

"Not surprising." Her lips pursed as she sorted through more receipts. "I never put any stock in that business. Bianca's tower was one thing. I guess we've all felt something—well, something up there. But I always thought that it was because we knew Bianca had tossed herself out of the window. Then last night..." When the shiver caught her, she rubbed her chilled arms. "I know that you really saw something, really experienced something."

"I know the necklace is real," C.C. said.

"I'll agree it *was* real—especially when I have a receipt in my hand."

"Was and is. I don't think I would have seen it if it had been pawned or tossed into the sea. It might sound loony, but I know Bianca wants us to find it."

"It does sound loony." With a sigh, Amanda leaned back in the creaking chair. "And what's loonier is that I think so, too. I just hope nobody at the hotel finds out I'm spending my free time looking for a buried treasure because my long-dead ancestor told us to. Oh!"

"Did you find it?" C.C. was already scrambling up.

"No, no, it's an old date book. 1912. The ink's a bit faded, but the handwriting's lovely—definitely feminine. It must be Bianca's. Look. 'Send invitations.' And here's the guest list. Wow, some party. The

Prentises." Amanda took off her glasses to gnaw on the earpiece. "I bet they were Prentise Hall—one of the cottages that burned in '47."

"'Speak to gardener about roses,'" C.C. read over her sister's shoulder. "'Final fitting on gold ball gown. Meet Christian, 3:00 p.m.' Christian?" She laid a tensed hand on Amanda's shoulder. "Could that have been her artist?"

"Your guess is as good as mine." Quickly Amanda pushed her glasses back on. "But look here. 'Have clasp on emeralds strengthened.' Those could be the ones."

"They have to be."

"We still haven't found any receipts."

C.C. gave a tired look at the papers littering the room. "What are our chances?"

Even Amanda's organizational skills quaked. "Well, they improve every time we eliminate a box."

"Mandy." C.C. sat on the floor beside her. "We're running out of time, aren't we?"

"We've only been at it for a few hours."

"That's not what I mean." She rested her cheek on Amanda's thigh. "You know it's not. Even if we find the receipt, we still have to find the necklace. It could take years. We don't have years. We're going to have to sell, aren't we?"

"We'll talk about it tomorrow night, at the family meeting." Troubled, she stroked C.C.'s hair. "Look, why don't you go take a nap? You really do look beat."

"No." She rose, pacing over the papers to the windows and back. "I'm better off keeping my mind and my hands busy. Otherwise, I might strangle someone."

"Trent, for instance?"

"An excellent place to start. No." With a sigh, she stuck her hands into her pockets. "No, this mess isn't really his fault."

"Are we still talking about the house?"

"I don't know." Miserable, she sat on the floor again. At least she could be grateful she'd cried herself dry the night before. "I've decided that all men are stupid, selfish and totally unnecessary."

"You're in love with him."

A wry smile curved her lips. "Bingo. And to answer your next question, no, he doesn't love me back. He's not interested in me, a future, a family, and he's very sorry he didn't make that clear to me before I made the mistake of falling for him."

"I'm sorry, C.C." After taking off her glasses, Amanda got up to cross the room and sit on the floor beside her sister. "I know how it must hurt, but you've only known him for a few days. Infatuation—"

"It's not infatuation." Idly she folded the recipe for jam into a paper airplane. "I've found out that falling in love doesn't have anything to do with time. It can take a year or an instant. It happens when it's ready to happen."

Amanda put an arm around C.C.'s shoulders and squeezed. "Well, I don't know anything about that. Fortunately, I've never had to worry about it." The fact made her frown, but only for a moment. "I do know this. If he hurt you, we'll make him sorry he ever crossed a Calhoun."

C.C. laughed then sent the gooseberry plane flying. "It's tempting, but I think it's more a matter of me hurting myself." She gave herself a little shake. "Come on, let's get back to work."

They'd barely gotten started again when Trent came in. He looked at C.C., met a solid wall of ice. When he turned to Amanda, he fared little better.

"I thought you might be able to use some help," he told them.

Amanda glanced at C.C., noted her sister was employing the silent treatment. A very effective weapon, in Amanda's estimation. "That's nice of you, Trent." Amanda gave him a smile that would have frosted molten lava. "But this is really a family problem."

"Let him help." C.C. didn't even bother to look up. "I imagine he's just terrific at pushing papers."

"All right then." With a shrug, Amanda indicated another folding chair. "You can use that if you like. I'm organizing according to content and year."

"Fine." He took the chair and sat across from her. They worked in frigid silence, with the crinkle of papers and the tap of Amanda's shoe.

"Here's a repair bill," he said—and was ignored. "For repairing a clasp."

"Let me see." Amanda had already snatched it out of his hand before C.C. made the dash across the room. "It doesn't say what kind of necklace," she muttered.

"But the dates are right." C.C. stabbed a finger on it. "July 16, 1912."

"Have I missed something?" Trent asked them.

Amanda waited a beat, saw that C.C. wasn't going to answer and glanced up herself. "We came across a date book of Bianca's. She had a note to take the emeralds to have the clasp repaired."

"This might be what you need." His eyes were on C.C., but it was Amanda who answered.

"It may be enough to satisfy all of us that the Calhoun necklace existed in 1912, but it's a long way from helping us find it." She set the receipt aside. "Let's see what else we can turn up."

In silence, C.C. went back to her papers.

A few moments later, Lilah called from the base of the stairs. "Amanda! Phone!"

"Tell them I'll call back."

"It's the hotel. They said it's important."

"Damn." She set down the glasses before sending Trent a narrowed look. "I'll be back in a few minutes."

He waited until the sound of her rapid footsteps had finished echoing. "She's very protective."

"We stick together," C.C. commented, and set a paper on a pile without a clue to its contents.

"I've noticed. Catherine..."

Braced, C.C. flicked him her coolest glance. "Yes?"

"I wanted to make certain you were all right."

"All right. In what way?"

She had dust on her cheek. He wanted, badly, to smile and tell her. To hear her laugh as she brushed it off. "After last night—I know how upset you were when you left my room."

"Yes, I was upset." She turned over another piece of paper. "I guess I made quite a scene."

"No, that's not what I meant."

"I did." She forced her lips to curve. "I guess I'm the one who should apologize this time. The séance, all that happened during it, went to my head." Not my head, she thought, but my heart. "I must have sounded like an idiot when I came to your room."

"No, of course not." She was so cool, he thought. So composed. And she baffled him. "You said you loved me."

"I know what I said." Her voice dropped another ten degrees, but her smile stayed in place. "Why don't we both chalk it up to the mood of the moment?"

That was reasonable, he realized. So why did he feel so lost. "Then you didn't mean it?"

"Trent, we've only known each other for a few days." Did he want to make her suffer? she wondered.

"But you looked so—devastated when you left."

She arched a brow. "Do I look devastated now?"

"No," he said slowly. "No, you don't."

"Well, then. Let's forget it." As she spoke, the sun lost itself behind the clouds. "That would be best for both of us, wouldn't it?"

"Yes." It was just what he'd wanted. Yet he felt empty when he stood up again. "I do want what's best for you, C.C."

"Fine." She studied the paper in her hand. "If you're going down, ask Lilah to bring up some coffee when she comes."

"All right."

She waited until she was sure he was gone before she covered her face with her hands. She'd been wrong, C.C. discovered. She hadn't nearly cried herself dry.

Trent went back to his room. His briefcase was there, stacked with work he had intended to do while away from his office. Taking a seat at the scarred kneehole desk, he opened a file.

Ten minutes later, he was staring out the window without having glanced at the first word.

He shook himself, picked up his pen and ordered himself to concentrate. He succeeded in reading the first word, even the first paragraph. Three times. Disgusted, he tossed the pen aside and rose to pace.

It was ridiculous, he thought. He had worked in hotel suites all over the world. Why should this room be any different? It had walls and windows, a ceiling—so to speak. The desk was more than adequate. He could even, if he chose, light a fire to add some cheer. And some warmth. God knew he could use some warmth after the thirty icy minutes he'd spent in the storeroom. There was no reason why he shouldn't be able to sit down and take care of some business for an hour or two.

Except that he kept remembering—how lovely C.C. had looked when she'd come into the room in her gray flannel robe and bare feet. He could still see the way her eyes had glowed when she had stood almost where he was standing now, smiling at him. Frowning, he rubbed at a dull pain around his heart. He wasn't accustomed to aches there. Headaches certainly. Never heartaches.

But the memory of the way she'd slipped into his arms haunted him. And her taste—why was it that it still hovered just a breath from his own lips?

It was guilt, that was all, he assured himself. He had hurt her, the way he was certain he'd never hurt another woman. No matter how cool she had been to-day, no matter how composed, that was a guilt he would live with for a long time.

Maybe if he went up and talked to her again. His hand was on the knob before he stopped himself. That would only make things worse, if possible. Just because he wanted to assuage some guilt was no excuse to put her in an uncomfortable position again.

She was handling it, better than he by all accounts. She was strong, obviously resilient. Proud. Soft, his mind wandered. Warm. Incredibly beautiful.

On an oath he began to pace again. It would be wiser for him to concentrate on the house rather than any of its occupants. The few days he'd spent in it might have caused a personal upheaval, but it had given him time and opportunity to formulate plans. From the inside. It had given him a taste of the mood and tone and the history. And if he could settle down for a few moments, he could put some of those thoughts on paper.

But it was hopeless. The minute he took his pen in hand, his mind went blank. He was feeling closed in, Trent told himself. He just needed some air. Snatching up a jacket, he did something he hadn't given himself time to do in months.

He took a walk.

Following instinct, he headed toward the cliffs. Down the uneven lawn, around a crumbling stone wall. Toward the sea. The air had a bite. It seemed that spring had decided to pick up her pretty skirts and retreat. The sky was gray and moody, with a few hopeful patches of blue. Wildflowers that had been brave enough to shove their way through rock and soil blew fitfully in the wind.

Trent walked with his hands in his pockets, and his head down. Depression wasn't a familiar sensation, and he was determined to walk it off. When he glanced back, he could just see the peaks of towers above and behind. He turned away and faced the sea—unknowingly mirroring the stance of a man who had painted there decades before.

Breathtaking. It was the only word that came to his mind. Rocks tumbled dizzily down, pink and gray where the wind buffeted them, black where the water struck and funneled. Bad-tempered whitecaps churned, slicing at the darker water. Smoky fog rolled and shredded, and the air held a fresh threat of rain.

It should have been gloomy. It was simply spectacular.

He wished she was with him. That she would be here, now, beside him before time passed or the wind changed. She would smile, he thought. Laugh, as she planted those long, gorgeous legs and lifted her face to the blow. If she had been there, the beauty of it wouldn't make him feel so lonely. So damned lonely.

The tingle at the base of his neck had him turning, nearly reaching out. He'd been so certain that he would look and see her walking toward him. There was nothing but the slope of rock, and the wind. Yet the feeling of another presence remained, very real, so that he almost called out.

He was a sensible man, Trent assured himself. He knew he was alone. Yet it seemed as though someone was there with him, waiting. Watching. For a moment, he was certain he caught the light, drifting scent of honeysuckle.

Imagination, he decided, but his hand wasn't quite steady as he lifted it to push the blowing hair out his eyes.

Then there was weeping. Trent froze as he listened to the sad, quiet sound that sobbed just under the wind. It ebbed and flowed, like the sea itself. Something clenched inside his stomach as he strained to hear—though common sense told him there could be nothing to hear.

A nervous breakdown? he wondered. But the sound was real, damn it. Not a hallucination. Slowly, ears pricked, he climbed down a jumble of rocks.

"Who's there?" he shouted as the sound sighed and drifted on the wind. Chasing it, he hurried down, driven by an urgency that drummed through his blood. A shower of loose stones rattled into space, bringing him sharply back to reality.

What in God's name was he doing? Scrambling down a cliff wall after a ghost? He lifted his hands and saw that despite the brisk wind his palms were sweating. All he could hear now was the frantic pounding of his own heart. After forcing himself to stand still and take a few calming breaths, he looked around for the easiest form of assent.

He had just started back when the sound came again. Weeping. No, he realized. Whimpering. It was quite clear now and nearly under his feet. Crouching, Trent searched behind an outcrop of rock. It was a poor, pitiful sight, he thought. The little black puppy was hardly more than a ball of fur-covered bones. Relief poured through him, making him laugh out loud. He wasn't going crazy after all. As Trent studied it, the terrified pup tried to inch back, but there was nowhere to go. Its little frightened eyes fixed on Trent as it trembled. "Had a rough time, have you?" Cautiously Trent reached out, ready to snatch his hand back if the pup snapped. Instead it simply cowered and whined. "It's okay, fella. Relax. I won't hurt you." Gently he stroked the puppy between the ears with his fingertips. Still shivering, the pup licked Trent's hand. "Guess you're feeling pretty lonely." He sighed as he calmed the dog. "Me, too. Why don't we go back to the house?" He gathered the dog up, zipping it inside his jacket for the climb. When he was halfway to the top, Trent stopped then turned blindly around. It was at least fifty yards from where he had stood looking out to sea to where he had discovered the stray. His palms grew damp again when he realized it would have been impossible for him to have heard the puppy's whines from the ridge above. The distance and the wind would have smothered the whimpers. Yet he had heard...something. And, hearing it, had climbed down to find the lost dog. "What the devil was it?" Trent murmured, and cuddling the pup closer, headed for home. He was just beginning to feel foolish when he crossed the lawn. What was he supposed to say to his hostesses? Look what followed me home? How about—Guess what? I decided to take my life in my hands and climb back down the cliff. Look what I found. Neither opening seemed quite suitable. The sensible thing would be to get in the car and drive the dog down to the village. There was bound to be an animal shelter or vet. He could hardly march into the parlor and dump his find on the rug. But he couldn't, Trent discovered. He simply couldn't turn the shivering ball of fur over to strangers. The little guy trusted him and was even now curling softly under his heart. As he stood hesitating, C.C. came out of the house.

Trent shifted and tried to look natural. "Hi."

'Hi.'' She paused to button her denim jacket. "We're out of milk. Do you need anything from the village?"

A can of dog food, he thought, and cleared his throat. "No, thanks. I, ah..." The pup wriggled against his shirt. "Did you find anything?"

"Lots of things, but nothing that tells us where to look for the necklace." Her misery turned to curiosity as she watched the ripples run along his jacket. "Is everything all right?"

"Fine. Just fine." Trent cleared his throat, folded his arms. "I took a walk."

"Okay." It was awful, she thought, just awful. He could hardly meet her eyes. "Aunt Coco's making a light lunch if you're hungry."

"Oh—thanks."

She started to move by him when a high-pitched yip stopped her in her tracks. "What?"

"Nothing." He smothered an involuntary chuckle as the puppy wiggled along his ribs.

"Are you all right?"

"Yes, yes, I'm fine." He gave her a sheepish smile as the dog poked his nose above the zipper of the jacket.

"What have you got?" C.C. forgot her vow to keep her distance and stepped closer to tug the zipper down. "Oh! Trent, it's a puppy."

"I found him down in the rocks," he began quickly. "I wasn't sure just what to—"

"Oh, you poor little thing." She was already cooing as she gathered the puppy to her. "Are you lost?" She rubbed her cheek over its fur, nuzzled nose to nose. "There now, it's all right." The puppy wagged his tail so fast and hard he nearly fell out of her grip.

"Cute, isn't he?" Grinning, Trent moved closer to stroke. "Looks like he's been on his own for a while."

"He's just a baby." She crooned and cuddled. "Where did you say you found him?"

"Down on the rocks. I was walking." And thinking of you. Before he could stop himself, Trent reached out to touch her hair. "I couldn't just leave him there."

"Of course not." She looked up and saw that she was all but in his arms. His hand was in her hair, his eyes on hers.

"Catherine—"

The pup yipped again and had her jolting back. "I'll take him in. He must be cold, and hungry."

"All right." The only place left for his hands was his pockets. "Why don't I run down and get the milk?"

"Okay." Her smile was strained as she backed toward the steps. She turned and, murmuring to the puppy, dashed inside.

By the time Trent returned, the stray had a place of honor by the kitchen hearth and the undivided attention of four beautiful women.

"Wait until Suze and the kids get back," Amanda was saying. "They'll flip. He sure goes for your liver pâté, Aunt Coco."

"Obviously a gourmet among dogs." Lilah, already on her hands and knees, leaned her nose against his. "Aren't you, cutie?"

"I'm sure he should have something more bland." Coco was also on the floor, charmed. "With the proper care, he'll be very handsome."

The pup, amazed at his good fortune, raced in circles. Spotting Trent, he gamboled over, tripping over his own feet. The women scrambled up, all asking him questions at the same time.

"Hold on." Trent set the grocery bag on the table, then crouched down to scratch the pup's belly. "I don't know where he came from. I found him when I was walking along the cliffs. He was hiding out. Weren't you, boy?"

"I suppose we should ask around, to see it anyone's lost him," Coco began, then held up a hand as her nieces voiced unanimous dissent. "It's only right. But it is up to Trent, since he found him."

"I think you should do what you think's best." He rose to pull the milk out of the bag. "He could probably use some of this."

Amanda already had a saucer and was arguing with Lilah on the proper amount to give their new guest.

"What else did you get?" C.C. poked at the bag.

"A few things." He moved his shoulders, then gave up. "I thought he should have a collar." Trent pulled out a bright red collar with silver studs.

C.C. couldn't hold back the grin. "Very fashionable."

"And a leash." Trent set that on the table, as well. "Puppy food."

"Uh-huh." C.C. began to go through the bag herself. "And puppy treats, rawhide bones."

"He'll want to gnaw," Trent told her.

"Sure, he will. A ball and a squeaky mouse." Laughing, she squeezed the rubber toy.

"He should have something to play with." He didn't want to add that he'd searched for a dog bed and cushion but hadn't come across them.

"I didn't know you were a softie."

He glanced down at the happily lapping puppy. "Neither did I."

"What's his name?" Lilah wanted to know.

"Well, I . . ."

"You found him, you get to name him."

"Do it quick," Amanda advised him. "Before Lilah sticks him with something like Griswold."

"Fred," Trent said on impulse. "He looks like a Fred to me."

Unimpressed with his christening, Fred plopped down with one ear in the saucer of milk and went to sleep.

"Well, that's settled." Amanda gave the pup one last pat before she rose. "Come on, Lilah, it's your turn to take a shift."

"I'll give you a hand." Instincts humming, Coco hustled her two nieces out of the room and left C.C. alone with Trent.

"I'd better go, too." C.C. started for the door. Trent laid a hand on her arm to stop her.

"Wait."

"What for?"

"Just . . . wait."

She stood, battling back hurt. "I'm waiting."

"I—how's your hand?"

"It's fine."

"Good." He felt like an idiot. "That's good."

"If that's all . . ."

"No. I wanted to tell you . . . I noticed a rattle in the car when I drove down to the village."

"A rattle?" She pursed her lips. "What kind of rattle?"

An imaginary one, he thought, but shrugged. "Just a rattle. I was hoping you could take a look at it."

"All right. Bring it in tomorrow."

"Tomorrow?"

"My tools are at the shop. Is there anything else?"

"When I was walking, I kept wishing you were with me."

She looked away until she was sure she had rebuilt the chink he'd just knocked in her defensive wall. "We want different things, Trent. Let's just leave it at that." She turned toward the door. "Try to get your car in early," she added without looking around. "I've got an exhaust system to replace tomorrow."

Chapter Eight

C.C. fired up her torch, flipped down her faceplate and prepared to cut off the tail pipe on the rusted exhaust of a '62 Plymouth.

The day was not going well.

She wasn't able to get the scheduled family meeting off her mind. No other paperwork on the necklace had shown up, though they had gone through reams and reams of receipts and old ledgers. She knew, because of Amanda's refusal to talk, that the news wasn't good.

Added to that had been another restless night. She heard Fred's whimpering and had gone to check on him only to hear Trent's low murmuring soothing the puppy behind his bedroom door.

She'd stood there for a long time, listening.

The fact that he'd taken the stray into his room, cared enough to comfort and nurture only made C.C.

love him more. And the more she loved, the more she hurt.

She knew she was hollow eyed this morning, because she'd made the mistake of looking at a mirror. That she could handle. Her looks had never been a major concern. The bills she had found in the morning mail were.

She'd been telling the truth when she'd told Suzanna the business was doing well. But there were still rough spots. Not all of her customers paid promptly, and her cash flow was too often merely a trickle. Six months, she thought as she cut through the old metal. She only needed six months. But that was too long, much too long to help keep The Towers.

Her life was changing, changing fast, and none of it seemed to be for the better.

Trent stood watching her. She had some battered hulk of a car up on the lift and stood under it, wielding a torch. While he watched, she shifted aside as a pipe clattered to the floor. She was wearing coveralls again, thick safety gloves and a helmet. The music she never seemed to be without jingled from the radio on the workbench.

Surely a man was over the edge when he thought how delightful it would be to make love on a concrete floor with a woman who was dressed like a welder.

C.C. changed positions, then saw him. Very carefully she shut off the torch before she lifted the shield of her helmet.

"I couldn't find anything wrong with your car. Keys are in the office. No charge." She flipped down the shield again.

"C.C."

"What?"

"How about dinner?"

She pushed back the shield and eyed him warily. "How about it?"

"I mean..." With a leery glance overhead, he stepped under the car with her. "I'd like you to have dinner with me tonight."

She shifted her weight. "I've had dinner with you every night for several nights." She flipped the shield down. Trent flipped it up again.

"No, I mean I want to take you out to dinner."

"Why?"

"Why not?"

She lifted a brow. "Well, that's very nice, but I'm a little pressed tonight. We're having a family meeting." She pulled down the shield again and prepared to relight the torch.

"Tomorrow then." Annoyed, Trent pushed the shield back up. "Do you mind? I like to see you when I talk to you."

"Yes, I mind because I've got work. And no, I won't have dinner with you tomorrow."

"Why?"

She blew out a long breath that ruffled her bangs. "Because I don't want to."

"You're still angry with me."

Her eyes, which had begun to heat, went flat. "We settled all that, so there's no reason to go out on a date."

"Just dinner," he said, finding he couldn't let go. "No one's calling it a date. One simple meal, as friends, before I go back to Boston."

"You're going back?" She felt her heart drop to her knees and turned away to rattle through some tools.

"Yes, I have meetings scheduled for the middle of the week. I'm expected in the office Wednesday afternoon."

Just like that, she thought as she picked up a pipe wrench and set it down again. I've got meetings scheduled, see you later. Sorry I broke your heart. "Well, then, have a nice trip."

"C.C." He laid a hand on her arm before she could hide behind the shield again. "I'd like to spend a little time with you. I'd feel a lot better about everything if I was sure we parted on good terms."

"You want to feel better about things," she muttered, then made herself relax her jaw. "Sure, why not? Dinner tomorrow night is fine. You deserve a send-off."

"I appreciate it. Really." He touched her cheek, started to lean toward her. C.C. pulled the shield down with a snap.

"Better stand back from the torch, Trent," she said sweetly. "You might get burned."

Family meetings with the Calhouns were traditionally noisy, argumentative and drenched with tears and laughter. This one was abnormally subdued. Amanda, in her capacity as adviser on finances, sat at the head of the table.

The room was silent.

Suzanna had already put the children to bed. It had been a little easier than usual as both of them had exhausted themselves with Fred—and vice versa.

Trent had excused himself discreetly, directly after dinner. It hardly mattered, C.C. thought. He would know the outcome soon enough.

She was afraid everyone knew it already.

"I guess we all know why we're here," Amanda began. "Trent's going back to Boston on Wednesday, and it would be best all around it we gave him our decision about the house before he left."

"It would be better if we concentrated on finding the necklace." Lilah's stubborn look was offset by the nervous way she twisted the obsidian crystals around her neck.

"We're all still looking for the papers." Suzanna laid a hand on Lilah's arm. "But I think we have to face the reality that finding the necklace could take a long time. Longer than we have."

"Thirty days is longer than we have." All eyes turned to Amanda. "I got a notice from the lawyer last week."

"Last week!" Coco put in. "Stridley contacted you and you didn't mention it?"

"I was hoping I could get an extension without worrying everyone." Amanda laid her hand on the file she set on the table. "No deal. We've been chipping away at the back taxes, but the hard fact is that we haven't been making enough headway. The insurance premiums are due. We can make them all right, and the mortgage—for the time being. The utility bills over the winter were higher than usual, and the new furnace and repairs to the roof ate up a lot of our principal."

C.C. held up a hand. "How bad is it?"

"As bad as it gets." Amanda rubbed at an ache in her temple. "We could sell off a few more pieces, and keep our head above water. Just. But taxes are due again in a couple months, and we'll be back where we started."

"I can sell my pearls," Coco began, and Lilah cut her off.

"No. Absolutely not. We agreed a long time ago that there were some things that couldn't be sold. If we're going to face facts," she said grimly, "then let's face them."

"The plumbing's shot," Amanda continued, and had to clear her tightening throat. "If we don't get the rewiring done, we could end up burning the place down around our ears. Suzanna's lawyer's fees—"

"That's my problem," Suzanna interrupted.

"That's *our* problem," Amanda corrected, and got a unanimous note of assent. "We're a family," she continued. "We've been through the very worst together, and we handled it. Six or seven years ago, it looked as if everything was going to be fine. But... taxes have gone up, along with the insurance, the repairs, everything. It's not as though we're paupers, but the house eats up every cent of spare cash, and then some. If I thought we could weather this, hang in for another year or two, I'd say sell the Limoges, or a few antiques. But it's like trying to plug a hole in a dam and watching others spring out while your fingers are slipping."

"What are you saying, Mandy?" C.C. asked her.

"I'm saying." Amanda pressed her lips together. "I'm saying the only realistic choice I see is for us to sell the house. With the offer from St. James, we can pay off the debts, keep most of what's important to all of us and buy another. If we don't sell, it's going to be taken away from us in any case within a few months." A tear trickled down her cheek. "I'm sorry. I just can't find a way out."

"It's not your fault." Suzanna reached out for her hand. "We all knew it was coming."

Amanda sniffled and shook her head. "What buffer we had, we lost in the stock market crash. We just haven't been able to recover. I know I made the investments—"

"*We* made the investments." Lilah leaned over to join hands, as well. "On the recommendation of a very reputable broker. If the bottom hadn't fallen through, if I'd won the lottery, if Bax hadn't been such a greedy bastard, maybe things would be different now. But they're not."

"We'll still be together." Coco added her hand. "That's what matters."

"That's what matters," C.C. agreed, and laid her hand on top. And that, if nothing else, felt right. "What do we do now?"

Struggling for composure, Amanda sat back. "I guess we ask Trent to come down and make sure the offer still stands."

"I'll get him." C.C. pushed away from the table to walk blindly from the room.

She couldn't believe it. Even as she walked through the huddle of rooms, into the hallway, up the steps with her hand trailing along the banister, she couldn't believe it. None of it would be hers much longer.

There would come a time very soon when she wouldn't be able to step from her room onto the high stone terrace and look out at the sea. She wouldn't be able to climb the steps to Bianca's tower and find Lilah curled on the window seat, dreaming out through the dusty glass. Or Suzanna working in the garden with the children racing on the lawn nearby. Amanda wouldn't come bolting down the stairs in a hurry to get somewhere, do something. Aunt Coco would no longer fuss over the stove in the kitchen.

In a matter of moments, the life she'd known was over. The one to come had yet to begin. She was somewhere in a kind of limbo, too stunned from the loss to ache.

Trent crouched beside the fire where Fred snored on the bright red cushion in his new wicker dog bed. He was going to miss the little devil, Trent realized. Even if he had the time or inclination for a pet back in Boston, he didn't have the heart to take Fred away from the children, or from the women, if it came to that.

He'd seen C.C. tossing the ball for the pup in the side yard that afternoon when she'd come home from work. It had been so good to hear her laugh, to see her wrestle with the dog and Suzanna's children.

Oddly it reminded him of the image he'd had— daydream, he corrected. The daydream he'd had when his mind had wandered the night of the séance. Of him and C.C. sitting on a sunny porch, watching children play in the yard.

It was foolishness, of course, but something had tugged at him that afternoon when he'd stood at the door and looked at her tossing a ball to Fred. A good something, he remembered, until she'd turned and had seen him. Her laughter had died, and her eyes had gone cool.

He straightened, studying the flames in the fire. It was crazy, but he wished with his whole heart that she would flare up, just once more. Throw another punch at him. Call him names. The worst kind of punishment was her steady, passionless politeness.

The sound of the knock on the door had Fred yipping quietly in his sleep. When Trent answered, finding C.C. on the other side of the threshold, twin twinges of delight and distress danced through his system. He wouldn't be able to turn her away this time. It wouldn't be possible to tell her, or himself, that it couldn't be. He had to... Then he looked into her eyes.

"What's wrong? What's happened?" He reached out to comfort, but she stepped stiffly away.

"We'd like you to come downstairs, if you don't mind."

"Catherine—" But she was already walking away, her stride lengthening in her hurry for distance.

He found them all gathered around the dining room table, their faces composed. He was astute enough to understand that he was facing one combined will.

The Calhouns had closed ranks.

"Ladies?"

"Trent, sit down, please." Coco gestured to the chair beside her. "I hope we didn't disturb you?"

"Not at all." He looked at C.C., but she was staring fixedly at the wall above his head. "Are we having another séance?"

"Not this time." Lilah nodded toward Amanda. "Mandy?"

"All right." She took a deep breath and was relieved when Suzanna's hand gripped hers under the table. "Trent, we've discussed your offer for The Towers, and have decided to accept it."

He gave her a blank look. "Accept it?"

"Yes." Amanda pressed her free hand to her quivering stomach. "That is, if your offer still stands."

"Yes, of course it does." He scanned the room, his gaze lingering on C.C. "You're certain you want to sell?"

"Isn't that what you wanted?" C.C.'s voice was clipped. "Isn't that what you came for?"

"Yes." But he'd gotten a great deal more than he'd bargained for. "My firm will be delighted to purchase the property. But . . . I want to be certain that you're all agreed. That this is what you want. All of you."

"We're all agreed." C.C. went back to staring at the wall.

"The lawyers will handle the details," Amanda began again. "But before we hand things over them, I'd like to review the terms."

"Of course." He named the purchase price again. Hearing it had tears burning in C.C.'s eyes. "There's no reason why we can't be flexible on the timing," he went on. "I realize you'll want to do some kind of inventory before you—relocate."

It was what they wanted, he reminded himself. It was business. It shouldn't make him feel as if he'd just crawled out from under a rock.

"I think we'd like to make the move quickly." Suzanna glanced around the table for confirmation. "As soon as we can find another house."

"If there's anything I can do to help you—"

"You've done enough," C.C. interrupted coolly. "We can take care of ourselves."

"I'd like to add a condition." Lilah leaned forward. "You're purchasing the house, and the land. Not the contents."

"No. Naturally the furniture, heirlooms, personal possessions remain yours."

"Including the necklace." She inclined her head. "Whether it's found before we leave, or after, the Calhoun necklace belongs to the Calhouns. I want that in writing, Trent. If anytime during your renovations, the necklace is recovered, it belongs to us."

"All right." The little clause would drive the lawyers crazy, he thought. But that was their problem. "I'll see that it's put in the contract."

"Bianca's tower." She spoke slowly, afraid her voice would break. "Be careful what you do with it."

"How about some wine?" Coco rose, hands fluttering. "We should have some wine."

"Excuse me." C.C. made herself stand slowly, fighting the impulse to race from the room. "If we're all through, I think I'll go up. I'm tired."

Trent stared after her, but Suzanna stopped him. "I don't think she'd be receptive right now. I'll go."

C.C. went to the terrace to lean out over the wall and let the cold wind dry the tears. There should be a storm, she thought. She wished there was a storm, something as angry and as passionate as her own heart.

Pounding a fist on the wall, she cursed the day she'd ever met Trent. He wouldn't take her love, but he would take her home. Of course, if he had accepted the first and returned it, he could never have taken the house.

"C.C." Suzanna stepped out to slip an arm around her shoulders. "It's cold. Why don't we go inside?"

"It's not right."

"No." She gathered her sister closer. "It's not."

"He doesn't even know what it means." She dashed the angry tears away. "He can't understand. He wouldn't want to."

"Maybe he doesn't. Maybe no one can but us. But it's not his fault, C.C. We can't blame him because we couldn't hang on." She looked away from the gardens she loved, toward the cliffs that always drew her. "I left here once before—it seems like a lifetime ago, but it was only seven years. Nearly eight now." She sighed. "I thought it was the happiest day of my life, leaving the island for my new home in Boston."

"You don't have to talk about that. I know it hurts you."

"Not as much as it once did. I was in love, C.C., a new bride with the future in the palm of my hand. And when I turned around and saw The Towers disappearing behind me, I cried like a baby. I thought it would be easier this time." As tears threatened, she closed her eyes. "I wish it were. What is it about this place that pulls us so?" she wondered.

"I know we can find another house." C.C. linked fingers with her sister. "I know we'll be all right, even happy. But it hurts. And you're right, it's not Trent's fault. But..."

"You have to blame someone." Suzanna smiled.

"He hurt me. I really hate to admit that, but he hurt me. I want to be able to say that he made me fall in love with him. Even that he let me fall in love with him. But I did it all by myself."

"And Trent?"

"He isn't interested."

"From the way he looks at you, I'd say you're wrong."

"Oh, he's interested," C.C. said grimly. "But love has nothing to do with it. He very politely refused to take advantage of my—my lack of experience, as he called it."

"Oh." Suzanna looked out toward the cliffs again. Rejection, she knew, was the sharpest blade of all. "It doesn't help much, but it might have been more difficult for you if he hadn't been—sensible."

"He's sensible, all right," C.C. said through her teeth. "And being a sensible and a civilized man, he'd like us to be friends. He's even taking me to dinner tomorrow so he can be certain I'm not pining away for him, and he can go back to Boston guilt free."

"What are you going to do?"

"Oh, I'll go to dinner with him. I can be just as damned civilized as he can." She set her chin. "And when I'm finished, he's going to be sorry he ever set eyes on Catherine Calhoun." She whirled toward her sister. "Do you still have that red dress? The beaded one that's cut down to sin?"

Suzanna's grin spread. "You bet I do."

"Let's go take a look at it."

Well, well, well, C.C. thought. What a difference a day and a tight silk dress could make. Lips pursed, she turned in front of the cracked cheval glass in the corner of her room. The dress was just a smidgen too small for her—even with the frantic alterations Suzanna had made. It only made more of a statement.

Don't you wish you had me, it said quite clearly. C.C. ran her hands over her hips. And he could wish until his head exploded.

The dress was a form-fitting glitter of flame that licked down from its plunging neckline to the abbreviated hem. Suzanna had ruthlessly slashed it off so that it hit C.C. midthigh. The long sleeves ended in points over her wrists. And she'd added Coco's rhinestone ear clips, with their wicked sparkle.

The thirty minutes she'd spent on makeup seemed to have paid off. Her lips were as red as the dress, thanks to Amanda's contribution. Her eyes were shadowed with copper and emerald, thanks to Lilah. Her hair was as glossy as a raven's wing and slicked back a bit at the temples.

All in all, C.C. thought as she turned, Trenton St. James III was in for a surprise.

"Suzanna said you needed some shoes." Lilah walked in and stopped in midyawn. The shoes dangled from her fingertips as she stared. "I must have passed through a parallel universe."

C.C. grinned and spun a circle. "What do you think?"

"I think Trent's going to need oxygen." Approving, she passed C.C. a pair of spiked snakeskin heels. "Kiddo, you look dangerous."

"Good." She pulled on the shoes. "Now if I can just walk in these without falling on my face."

"Practice. I've got to get Mandy."

A few moments later, all three sisters supervised C.C.'s walk. "You'll be having dinner," Amanda put in, wincing at each wobble. "So you'll be sitting down most of the time."

"I'm getting it," C.C. muttered. "I'm just not used to heels. How do you work in these things all day?"

"Talent."

"Walk slower," Lilah suggested. "More deliberately. As if you have all the time in the world."

"Take if from her," Amanda agreed. "She's an expert at slow."

"In this case—" Lilah gave Amanda an arched look "—slow is sexy. See?"

Taking her sister's advice, C.C. walked with a cautious deliberation that came off as slinky. Amanda held out her hands. "I stand corrected. What coat are you wearing?"

"I haven't thought of it."

"You can wear my black silk cape," Amanda decided. "You'll freeze but you'll look great doing it. Perfume. Aunt Coco's got some of that smoldering French stuff left from Christmas."

"No." Suzanna shook her head. "She should stick with her usual scent." Tilting her head, she studied her sister and smiled. "The contrast will drive him crazy."

Unaware of what was in store for him, Trent sat in the parlor with Coco. His bags were packed. His calls were made. He wished he could come up with a reasonable excuse to stay another few days.

"We've enjoyed having you," Coco told him when he'd expressed his appreciation for her hospitality. "I'm sure we'll be seeing each other again soon."

Her crystal ball didn't lie, she reminded herself. It still linked Trent up with one of her nieces, and she wasn't ready to wave surrender.

"I certainly hope so. I have to say, Coco, how much I admire you for raising four such lovely women."

"Sometimes I think we raised each other." She smiled mistily around the room. "I'm going to miss this place. To be honest I didn't think it mattered to me until...well, until now. I didn't grow up here as the girls did. We traveled quite a bit, you see, and my father only came back sporadically. I always thought it was the fact that his mother had died here that put him off. Then, of course, I spent my married life and the first few years of my widowhood in Philadelphia. Then when Judson and Deliah were killed, I came here for the girls." She sent him a sad, apologetic smile. "I'm sorry to get sentimental on you, Trenton."

"Don't apologize." He sipped thoughtfully at his aperitif. "My family has never been close, and as a result, there was never a home like this in my life. I think that's why I've begun to understand what it could mean."

"You should settle down," she said, cagily, she thought. "Find a nice girl, make a home and family of your own. Why, I can't think of anything lonelier than not having anyone to go home to."

Wanting to avoid that line of thought, he reached down to throw the ball for Fred. They both watched as the dog bounded after it, tripped himself up and went sprawling.

"Not particularly graceful," Trent mused. He rose and went over to retrieve the ball himself. Scratching the dog's belly, he glanced over. The first thing he saw was a pair of very slim black heels. Slowly his gaze traveled up a long, shapely pair of legs. With the breath backing up in his lungs, he sat back on his heels.

There was a sparkle of scarlet, snug and sleek over a curvy feminine form.

"Lose something?" C.C. asked as his eyes fixed on her face.

Her lips were curved and red and slick. Trent ran his tongue over his teeth to be certain he hadn't swallowed it. On unsteady legs, he rose.

"C.C.?"

"We were having dinner tonight, weren't we?"

"We . . . yes. You look wonderful."

"Do you like it?" She turned a circle so that he could see the back of the dress dipped even lower than the front. "I think red's a cheerful color." And powerful, she thought, still smiling.

"It suits you. I've never seen you in a dress before."

"Impractical when it comes to changing fuel pumps. Are you ready to go?"

"Go where?"

Oh, she was going to enjoy this. "To dinner."

"Right. Yes."

She inclined her head the way Suzanna had showed her and handed him her cape. It was a service he'd performed hundreds of times for dozens of women. But his hands fumbled.

"Don't wait up, Aunt Coco."

"No, dear." Behind their retreating backs, she grinned and raised her fists in the air. The moment the front door shut, the three remaining Calhouns exchanged high fives.

Chapter Nine

"I'm glad you talked me into going out tonight." C.C. reached for the door handle before she remembered to let Trent open the car for her.

"I wasn't sure you'd still be willing to go." He closed his hand over hers.

"Because of the house?" As casually as possible, C.C. slid her hand from under his and lowered herself into the car. "That's done. I'd rather not talk about it tonight."

"All right." He closed the door, rounded the hood. "Amanda recommended the restaurant." He had his hands on the keys but continued to stare at her.

"Something wrong?"

"No." Unless you counted his nervous system. After starting the car, he tried again. "I thought you might like dining near the water."

"Sounds fine." His radio was on a classical station. Not her usual style, she thought. But it wasn't a usual night. C.C. settled back and prepared to enjoy the ride. "Have you heard that rattle again?"

"What rattle?"

"The one you asked me to fix yesterday."

"Oh, that rattle." He smiled to himself. "No. It must have been my imagination." When she crossed her legs, his fingers tightened on the wheel. "You never told me why you decided to be a mechanic."

"Because I'm good at it." She shifted in her seat to face him. He caught a drift of honeysuckle and nearly groaned. "When I was six, I took apart our lawn mower's engine, to see how it worked. I was hooked. Why did you go into hotels?"

"It was expected of me." He stopped, surprised that that had been the first answer out of his mouth. "And I suppose I got good at it."

"Do you like it?"

Had anyone ever asked him that before? he wondered. Had he ever asked himself? "Yes, I guess I do."

"Guess?" Her brows lifted into her bangs. "I thought you were sure of everything."

He glanced at her again and nearly ran off the road. "Apparently not."

When they arrived at the waterfront restaurant, he was used to the transformation. Or thought he was. Then he went around to open the car door for her. She slid out, rose up. They were eye to eye, barely a whisper apart. C.C. held her ground, wondering if he could hear the way her heart was pounding against her ribs.

"Are you sure nothing's wrong?"

"No, I'm not sure." No one, he was certain, this impossibly sexy was meant to be resisted. He cupped a hand at the back of her neck. "Let me check."

She eased away the instant before his lips brushed hers. "This isn't a date, remember? Just a friendly dinner."

"I'd like to change the rules."

"Too late." She smiled and offered a hand. "I'm hungry."

"You're not the only one," he murmured, and took her inside.

He wasn't sure how to handle her. The smooth moves he'd always taken for granted seemed rusty. The setting was perfect, the little table beside the window with water lapping just outside. As the sun set away in the west, it deepened and tinted the bay. He ordered wine as she picked up her menu and smiled at him.

Under the table, C.C. gently eased out of her shoes. "I haven't been here before," she told him. "It's very nice."

"I can't guarantee the food will be as exceptional as your aunt's."

"No one cooks like Aunt Coco. She'll be sorry to see you go. She likes cooking for a man."

"Will you?"

"Will I what?"

"Be sorry to see me go."

C.C. looked down at the menu, trying to concentrate on her choices. The hard fact was, she had none. "Since you're still here, we'll have to see. I imagine you have a lot to catch up on in Boston."

"Yes, I do. I've been thinking that after I do, I may take a vacation. A real one. Bar Harbor might be a good choice."

She looked up, then away. "Thousands think so," she murmured, relieved when the waiter served the wine.

"If you could go anywhere you liked, where would it be?"

"That's a tough question, since I haven't been anywhere." She sipped, found the wine as smooth as chilled silk on her tongue. "Somewhere where I could see the sun set on the water, I think. Someplace warm." She shrugged. "I suppose I should have said Paris or London."

"No." He laid a hand on hers. "Catherine—"

"Are you ready to order?"

C.C. glanced quickly at the waiter who hovered beside them. "Yes." She slid her hand from Trent's and picked arbitrarily from the menu. Cautious, she kept one hand in her lap as she lifted her wine. The moment they were alone again, she started to speak. "Have you ever seen a whale?"

"I . . . no."

"You'll be coming back occasionally while you're—while you're having The Towers converted. You should take a day and go out on one of the whale-watch boats. The last time I managed it, I saw three humpback. You need to dress warmly though. Even in high summer it's cold once you get out on the Atlantic. It can be a rough ride, but it's worth it. You might even think about offering some sort of package yourself. You know, a weekend rate with a whale-watch tour included. A lot of the hotels—"

"Catherine." He stopped her by closing a hand over her wrist before she could lift her glass again. He could feel the rapid, unsteady beat of her pulse. Not passion this time, he thought. But heartache. "The papers haven't been signed yet," he said quietly. "There's still time to look for other options."

"There aren't any other options." He cared, she realized as she studied his face. It was in his eyes as they looked into hers. Concern, apology. It made it worse somehow, knowing he cared. "We sell to you now, or The Towers is sold later for taxes. The end result is the same, and there's a little more dignity doing it this way."

"I might be able to help. A loan."

She retreated instantly. "We can't take your money."

"If I buy the house from you, you're taking my money."

"That's different. That's business. Trent," she said before he could argue, "I appreciate the fact that you'd offer, especially since I know the only reason you're here is to buy The Towers."

It was, he thought. Or it had been. "The thing is, C.C., I feel like I'm foreclosing on those widows and orphans."

She managed a smile. "We're five strong, self-sufficient women. We don't blame you—or maybe I do, a little, but at least I know I'm being unfair when I do. My feelings for you don't make it easy to be fair.

"What are your feelings?"

She let out a little sigh as the waiter served the appetizers and lit the candle between them. "You're taking the house, you might as well take it all. I'm in love with you. But I'll get over it." With her head tilted slightly, she lifted her fork. "Is there anything else you want to know?"

When he took her hand again, she didn't pull back, but waited. "I never wanted to hurt you," he said carefully. How well her hand fit into his, he thought, looking down at it. How comforting it was to link his fingers with hers. "I'm just not capable of giving you—of giving anyone—promises of love and fidelity."

"That's sad." She shook her head as his eyes came back to hers. "You see, I'm only losing a house. I can find another. You're losing the rest of your life, and you only have one." She forced her lips to curve as she drew away from him. "Unless, of course, you subscribe to Lilah's idea that we just keep coming back. This is nice wine," she commented. "What is it again?"

"Pouilly Fumé."

"I'll have to remember that." She began to talk cheerfully as she ate the meal without tasting a thing. By the time coffee was served, she was wound like a top. C.C. knew that she would rather take an engine apart with her fingernails than face another evening such as this.

To love him so desperately, yet to have to be strong enough, proud enough to pretend she was capable of living without him. To sit, greedily storing each gesture, each word, while pretending it was all so casual and easy.

She wanted to shout at him, to rage and damn him for stirring her emotions into a frenzy then calmly walking away from the storm. But she could only cling to the cold comfort of pride.

"Tell me about your home in Boston," she invited. That would be something, she thought, to be able to picture him in his own home.

He wasn't able to take his eyes off her. The way the clusters at her ears shot fire. The way the candlelight flickered dreamily in her eyes. But all through the evening, he had felt as though she had blocked off a part of herself, the most important part of herself. And he might never see the whole woman again.

"My home?"

"Yes, where you live."

"It's just a house." It occurred to him quite suddenly that it didn't mean a thing to him. An excellent investment, that was all. "It's only a few minutes from the office."

"That's convenient. Have you lived there long?"

"About five years. Actually, I bought it from my father when he and his third wife split. They decided to liquidate some assets."

"I see." And she was very much afraid that she did. "Does your mother live in Boston, too?"

"No. She travels. Being tied down to one place doesn't agree with her."

"Sounds like Great-Aunt Colleen." C.C. smiled over the rim of her cup. "That's my father's aunt, or Bianca's oldest child."

"Bianca," he mused, and thought again of that moment when he'd felt that soft and soothing warmth over his and C.C.'s joined hands.

"She lives on cruise ships. Every now and again we get a postcard from some port of call. Aruba or Madagascar. She's eighty-something, obsessively single and mean as a shark with a hangover. We all live in fear that she might decide to visit.''

''I didn't realize you had any relatives living other than Coco and your sisters.'' His brows drew together. ''She might know something about the necklace.''

''Great-Aunt Colleen?'' Considering it, C.C. pursed her lips. ''I doubt it. She was a child when Bianca died, and spent most of her girlhood in boarding schools.'' Without thinking, she pulled off her earrings and massaged the tender lobes. Desire spread like brushfire through Trent's blood. ''Anyway, if we could find her—which isn't likely—and mentioned the whole business, she'd probably come steaming back to hack away at the walls. She doesn't have any love for The Towers, but she has a great deal for money.''

''She doesn't sound like a relative of yours.''

''Oh, we have a number of oddities in our family closet.'' After dropping the earrings into her bag, she leaned an elbow on the table. ''Great-Uncle Sean—he was Bianca's youngest—was shot climbing out of his married paramour's window. One of his paramours, I should say. He survived, then took off for the West Indies, never to be heard from again. That was sometime during the thirties. Ethan, my grandfather, lost the bulk of the family fortune on cards and horses. Gambling was his weakness, and that's what killed him. He had a wager that he could sail from Bar Harbor to Newport and back within six days. He made it to Newport, and was heading back ahead of schedule when he ran into a squall and was lost at sea. Which meant he lost his last bet as well.''

"They sound like an adventurous pair."

"They were Calhouns," C.C. explained, as if that said it all.

"I'm sorry the St. Jameses don't have anything to compare with it."

"Ah, well. I've always wondered if Bianca would have stepped back from that tower window if she'd known how messed up her children would become." C.C. looked thoughtfully out to where lights played on the dark water. "She must have loved her artist very much."

"Or was very unhappy in her marriage."

C.C. looked back. "Yes, there is that. Maybe we should head back. It's getting late." She started to rise, remembered, then slid her bare foot around the floor beneath the table.

"What is it?"

"I've lost my shoes." So much, she thought, for the sophisticated image.

Trent bent down to look himself and got an eyeful of long, slim leg. "Ah..." He cleared his throat and trained his eyes on the floor. "Here you go." He took both, then straightening, smiled at her. "Put your foot out. I'll give you a hand." He watched her as he slipped the shoes onto her feet and remembered that he'd once thought she would never stand for being a Cinderella. He trailed his finger up her instep and caught the flicker in her eyes. The flicker of desire that, no matter what common sense told him, he very much wanted.

"Have I mentioned that you have truly incredible legs?"

"No." She had one hand balled in a fist at her side and struggled to concentrate on it rather than the sensations his touch had spurting through her. "It's nice of you to notice."

"It's difficult not to. They're the only ones I've known that look sexy in coveralls."

Ignoring the thud of her own heart, she leaned toward him. "That reminds me."

He could kiss her now, he thought. He had only to shift a mere inch to have his mouth on hers, where he wanted it. "What?"

"I don't think your shocks have more than another couple thousand miles on them." With a smile, she rose. "I'd look into that when you get home." Pleased with herself, C.C. started out ahead of him.

When they settled in the car, she congratulated herself. A very successful evening all in all, she thought. Maybe he wasn't miserable, as she was, but she was damn sure she'd made him uncomfortable a time or two. He'd go back to Boston the next day.... She turned to stare out the window until she was certain she could deal with the pain. He'd go back, but he wouldn't forget her quickly or easily. His last impression of her would be one of a composed, self-contained woman in a sexy red dress. Better, C.C. decided, much better than the picture of a mechanic in coveralls with grease on her hands.

More importantly, she'd proven something to herself. She could love, and she could let go.

She looked up as the car started to climb. She could see the shadowy peaks of the two towers spearing into the night sky. Trent slowed the car as he looked, as well.

"The light's on in Bianca's tower."

"Lilah," C.C. murmured. "She often sits up there." She thought of her sister sitting by the window, looking out into the night. "You won't tear it down, will you?"

"No." Understanding more than she knew, he closed his hand over hers. "I promise you it won't be torn down."

The house disappeared as the road curved away, then all but filled the view. They could hear the beat and slap of the sea as they looked at it. Lights were sprinkled on throughout, glowing against the dull gray stone. A slender shadow moved in front of the tower window, stood for a moment, then slid away.

Inside, Lilah called down the stairs. "They're back."

Four women raced to the windows to peer out.

"We shouldn't spy on them," Suzanna murmured, but moved the curtain aside a bit more.

"We're not." Amanda strained her eyes. "We're just checking, that's all. Can you see anything?"

"They're still in the car," Coco complained. "How are we supposed to see what's going on if they're going to sit in the car?"

"We could use our imaginations." Lilah shook her hair back. "If that man isn't begging her to go to Boston with him, then he really is a jerk."

"To Boston?" Alarmed, Suzanna glanced over. "You don't think she'd go to Boston, do you?"

"She'd go to the Ukraine if he had the sense to ask her," Amanda commented. "Look, they're getting out."

"Maybe if we just cracked a window a little bit, we could hear—"

"Aunt Coco, that's ridiculous." Lilah clucked her tongue.

"You're right, of course." Color tinged Coco's cheek.

"Of course I'm right. They'd hear the windows creak if we tried." Grinning, she pressed her face against the glass. "We'll just have to read their lips."

"This was nice," C.C. said as she stepped out of the car. "I haven't been out to dinner in a while."

"You had dinner with Finney."

She gave him a blank look, then laughed. "Oh, Finney, sure." The breeze played with her bangs as she smiled. "You've got quite a memory."

"Some things seem to stick to it." The jealousy he felt was, unfortunately, no memory. "Doesn't he ever take you out?"

"Finney? No, I just go to his place."

Frustrated, Trent jammed his hands into his pockets. "He should take you out."

She smothered a chuckle as the image of old Albert Finney escorting her to a restaurant ran through her mind. "I'll be sure to mention it to him." She turned to start up the steps.

"Catherine, don't go in yet." He took her hands.

At the windows four pairs of eyes narrowed.

"It's late, Trent."

"I don't know if I'll see you again before I leave."

It took all her strength to keep her eyes steady. "Then we'll say goodbye now."

"I need to see you again."

"The shop's open at eight-thirty. I'll be there."

"Damn it, C.C., you know what I mean." His hands were on her shoulders now.

"No, I don't."

"Come to Boston." He blurted it out, shocking himself while she stood calmly waiting.

"Why?"

To give himself a moment to find control again, he stepped back. "I could show you around." How much more inane could he get? Trent wondered. How much more beautiful could she look? "You said you'd never been. We could . . . have some time together."

Inside her wrap, she shivered, but her voice was calm and smooth. "Are you asking me to come to Boston and have an affair with you?"

"No. Yes. Oh, Lord. Just wait." He turned to pace a few steps away and breathe.

Inside, Lilah smiled. "Why, he's in love with her after all, but he's too stupid to know it."

"Shh!" Coco waved a hand. "I can almost hear what they're saying." She had an ear at the base of the water glass she pressed up to the window.

At the bottom of the steps, Trent tried again. "Nothing I begin ends the way I expect it to when I'm with you." He turned back. She was still standing with the house behind her, the dress glimmering like liquid fire in the dark. "I know I have no business asking you, and I didn't intend to. I intended to say a very civil goodbye and let you go."

"And now?"

"Now I want to make love with you more than I want to go on breathing."

"To make love," C.C. repeated steadily. "But you don't love me."

"I don't know anything about love. I care for you."
He walked back to touch a hand to her face. "Maybe
that could be enough."

She studied him, realizing he didn't have any idea
that he was breaking an already shattered heart. "It
might be, for a day or a week or a month. But you
were right about me, Trent. I expect more. I deserve
more." Keeping her eyes on his, she slid her hands
over his shoulders. "I offered myself to you once.
That won't happen again. And neither will this."

She pressed her mouth against his, pouring every
scrap of her tattered emotions into it. Her arms en-
folded him even as her body swayed seductively toward his. With a sigh, her lips parted, inviting him to
take.

Off balance, needy, he dragged her head back and
plundered. Unsteady, his hands skimmed beneath her
wrap, urgently seeking the warmth of her skin.

So many feelings, too many feelings, bombarded
him. He wanted only to fill himself with the taste of
her. But there was more. She wouldn't let him take
only the kiss, but all the emotion that went with it. He
felt he was drowning in it, but it was so strong and
heady a flood, he couldn't fight.

Love me! Why can't you love me? Her mind seemed
to scream it even as she was borne away on the tide of
her own longings. Everything she wanted was here,
inside the circle of her arms. Everything but his heart.

"Catherine." He couldn't get his breath. Dragging
her closer, he pressed his mouth to her neck. "I can't
get close enough."

She held him to her a moment longer, then slowly,
painfully, pulled away. "Yes, you could. And that's

what hurts the most." Turning, she dashed up the steps.

"Catherine."

She paused at the door. With her head high, she turned around. He was already coming after her when he saw the tears glittering in her eyes. Nothing else would have stopped him.

"Goodbye, Trent. I hope to God that keeps you up at night."

As he listened to the echo of the door slamming, he was certain it would.

It cannot go on. I can no longer pretend that I am disloyal to my husband only between the covers of this journal. My life, so calm and ordered during my twenty-four years, has become a lie this summer. One I must atone for.

As autumn approaches and we make our plans to return to New York, I thank God I will soon leave Mount Desert Island behind me. How close, how dangerously close I have come these past days to breaking my marriage vows.

And yet, I grieve.

In another week, we will be gone. I may never see Christian again. That is how it should be. How it must be. But in my heart I know that I would give my soul for one night, even one hour, in his arms. Imagining how it could be obsesses me. With him there would finally be passion, and love, even laughter. With him it would not simply be a duty, cold and silent and soon over.

I pray to be forgiven for the adultery I have committed in my heart.

My conscience has urged me to keep away from the cliffs. And I have tried. It has demanded that I be a more patient, loving and understanding wife to Fergus. I have done so. Whatever he has asked of me, I have done. At his request, I gave a tea for several of the ladies. We have gone to the theater, to countless dinner parties. I have listened until my head was throbbing to talk of business and fashion and the possibility of war. My smile never falters, for Fergus prefers that I look content at all times. Because it pleases him, I wear the emeralds when we go out in the evenings.

They are my penance now, a reminder that a sin is not always in the action, but in the heart.

I sit here in my tower now as I write. The cliffs are below, the cliffs where Christian paints. Where I go when I sneak from the house like a randy housemaid. It shames me. It sustains me. Even now I look down and see him. He faces the sea, and waits for me.

We have never touched, not once, though the ache is in both of us. I have learned how much passion there can be in silences, in long, troubled looks.

I will not go to him today, but only sit here and watch him. When I feel I have the strength, I will go to him only to say goodbye and wish him well.

While I live through the long winter that faces me, I will wonder if he will be here next summer.

Chapter Ten

"Here are the papers you asked for, Mr. St. James."

Oblivious to his secretary's presence, Trent continued to stand at the window, staring out. It was a habit he'd developed since returning to work three weeks before. Through the wide tinted glass, he could watch Boston bustling by below. Steel-and-glass towers glittered beside elegant brownstones in a architectural potpourri. Thick traffic weaved and charged on the streets. In sweats and colorful running shorts, joggers paced themselves along the path beside the river. Then there was the river itself, streaming with boats, sails puffed full of warm spring breezes.

"Mr. St. James?"

"Yes?" He glanced around at his secretary.

"I've brought you the papers you requested."

"Thank you, Angela." In an old habit, he looked at his watch. It occurred to him, painfully, that he had rarely thought of the time when he'd been with C.C. "It's after five. You should go home to your family."

Angela hesitated. She'd worked for Trenton for six years. It had only been during the past couple of weeks that he had begun calling her by her first name or inquiring about her family. The day before, he'd actually complimented her on her dress. The change in him had the entire staff baffled. As his secretary, she felt obligated to dig out the source of it.

"May I speak with you a minute?"

"All right. Would you like to sit down?"

"No, sir. I hope you won't consider this out of place, Mr. St. James, but I wanted to know if you're feeling well."

A ghost of a smile played around his mouth. "Don't I look well?"

"Oh, yes, of course. A little tired perhaps. It's just that since you returned from Bar Harbor, you seem distracted, and different somehow."

"You could say I am distracted. I am different, and to answer your original question, no, I don't think I am entirely well."

"Mr. St. James, if there's anything I can do..."

Studying her, he sat on the edge of his desk. He had hired her because she was efficient and quick. As he recalled, he had nearly passed her over because she'd had two small children. It had worried him that she wouldn't be able to balance her responsibilities, but he'd taken what he'd considered a chance. It had worked very well indeed.

"Angela, how long have you been married?"

"Married?" Thrown off, she blinked. "Ten years."

"Happily?"

"Yes, Joe and I are happy."

Joe, he mused. He hadn't even known her husband's name. Hadn't bothered to find it out. "Why?"

"Why, sir?"

"Why are you happy?"

"I . . . I suppose because we love each other."

He nodded, gesturing to prod her along. "And that's enough?"

"It certainly helps you get through the rough spots." She smiled a little, thinking of her Joe. "We've had some of them, but one of us always manages to pull the other through."

"You consider yourself a team then. So you have a great deal in common?"

"I don't know about that. Joe likes football and I hate it. He loves jazz, and I don't understand it." It wouldn't occur to her until later that this was the first time she'd felt completely at ease with Trent since she'd taken the job. "Sometimes I feel like wearing earplugs all weekend. Whenever I feel like shipping him out, I think about what my life would be without him. And I don't like what I see." Taking a chance, she stepped closer. "Mr. St. James, if this is about Marla Montblanc getting married last week, well, I'd just like to say that you're better off."

"Marla got married?"

Truly baffled, Angela shook her head. "Yes, sir. Last week, to that golf pro. It was in all the papers."

"I must have missed it." There had been other things in the papers that had captured his attention.

"I realize you'd been seeing her for quite a while."

Seeing her, Trent mused. Yes, that cool, passionless phrase described their relationship perfectly. "Yes, I had been."

"You're not—upset?"

"About Marla? No." The fact was he hadn't thought of her in weeks. Since he'd walked into a garage and spotted a pair of scarred boots.

Another woman, Angela realized. And if she'd had this kind of affect on the boss, she had all of Angela's support. "Sir, if someone—something else," she corrected cautiously, "is on your mind, you may be overanalyzing the situation."

The comment surprised him enough to make him smile again. "Do I overanalyze, Angela?"

"You're very meticulous, Mr. St. James, and analyze details finitely, which works very well in business. Personal matters can't always be dealt with logically."

"I've been coming to that same conclusion myself." He stood again. "I appreciate the time."

"My pleasure, Mr. St. James." And it certainly had been. "Is there anything else I can do for you?"

"No, thank you." He turned back to the window. "Good night, Angela."

"Good night." She was grinning when she closed the door at her back.

Trent stood where he was for some time. No, he hadn't noticed the announcement of Marla's wedding. The papers had also been full of the upcoming sale of The Towers. "Bar Harbor landmark to become newest St. James Hotel," he remembered. "Rumors of lost treasures sweeten the deal."

Trent wasn't certain where the leak had come from, though he wasn't surprised by it. As he'd expected, his lawyers had grumbled over the clause Lilah had insisted on. Whispers of emeralds had sneaked down the hallways. It was only natural that they would find their way onto the street and into print.

Newspapers and tabloids had been rife with speculation on the Calhoun emeralds for more than a week. They'd been termed priceless and tragic and legendary—all the right adjectives to ensure more newsprint.

Fergus Calhoun's business exploits had been rehashed, along with his wife's suicide. An enterprising reporter had even managed to track down Colleen Calhoun aboard a cruise ship in the Ionian Sea. The grande dame's pithy reply had been printed in italics.

"Humbug."

He wondered if C.C. had seen the papers. Of course, she had, he thought. Just as she'd probably been hounded by the press.

How was she taking it? Was she hurt and miserable, forced to answer questions when some nosy reporter stuck a tape recorder in her face? He smiled a little. *Forced?* He imagined she'd throw a dozen reporters out of the garage if they had the nerve to try.

God, he missed her. And missing her was eating him alive. He woke up each morning wondering what she was doing. He went to bed each night to toss restlessly as thoughts of her invaded his brain. When he slept, she was in his dreams. She was his dream.

Three weeks, he thought. He should have adjusted by now. Yet every day that he was here and she was somewhere else, it got worse.

The revised contracts for the sale of The Towers were sitting on his desk. He should have signed them days ago. Yet he couldn't make himself take that final step. The last time he had looked at them, he had only been able to focus on three words.

Catherine Colleen Calhoun.

He'd read it over and over, remembering the first time she'd told him her name, tossing it at him as though it had been a weapon. She'd had grease on her face, Trenton remembered. And fire in her eyes.

Then he would think of other times, odd moments, careless words. The way she had scowled at him from her perch on the arm of the sofa while he'd had tea with Coco. The look on her face when they'd stood on the terrace together, watching the sea. How perfectly her mouth had fit to his when he had kissed her under an arbor of wisteria not yet in bloom.

It would be blooming now, he mused. Those first fragrant flowers would be opening. Would she think of him at all when she walked there?

If she did, he was very much afraid the thoughts wouldn't be kind.

She'd cursed him when she'd seen him last. She'd leveled those deep green eyes at him and had hoped that the kiss, the last kiss they'd shared, would keep him up at night.

He doubted even she could know how completely her wish had come true.

Rubbing his tired eyes, he walked back to his desk. It was, as always, in perfect order. As his business was—as his life had been.

Things had changed, he was forced to admit. He had changed, but perhaps he hadn't changed so completely. Once again, he picked up the contracts to study them. He was still a skilled and organized businessman, one who knew how to maneuver a deal and make it work to his advantage.

He picked up his pen and tapped it lightly on the papers. A germ of an idea had rooted in his mind a few days before. Now he sat quietly and let it form, shift, realign.

It was unusual, he considered. Maybe even mildly eccentric, but... but, he thought as a smile began to curve his mouth, if he played his cards right, it could work. It was his job to make it work. Slowly he let out a long breath. It might just be the most important deal of his life.

He picked up the phone and, employing all of the St. James clout, began to turn the first wheels.

Hank finished sanding the fender on the '69 Mustang, then stood back to admire his work. "Coming along just fine," he called to C.C.

She glanced over, but her hands were full with the brake shoes she was replacing above her head. "It's going to be a beauty. I'm glad we got the shot at reconditioning it."

"You want me to start on the primer?"

She swore as brake fluid dripped onto her cheek. "No. You told me three times today that you've got a hot date tonight. Get cleaned up and take off."

"Thanks." But he'd been too well trained to leave without replacing tools and material. "You found another house yet?"

"No." She ignored the sudden ache in her stomach and concentrated on her work. "We're all going out tomorrow to look."

"Won't be the same, not having Calhouns in The Towers. Sure is something about that necklace, though. Papers are full of stories about it."

"They'll die down." She hoped.

"Guess if you find it, you'd be millionaires. You could retire and move to Florida."

Despite her mood, she had to chuckle. "Well, we haven't found it yet." Just the receipt, she mused, which Lilah had unearthed during her one and only shift in the storeroom. "Florida'll have to wait. The brakes won't."

"Guess I'll be going. Want me to lock up the office?"

"Go ahead. Have a good time."

He went out whistling, and C.C. stopped a moment to rest her arms and neck. She wished she'd been able to keep Hank around a while longer, for company, for the distraction. Even if he rambled on about the house and the necklace, he helped keep her mind occupied.

No matter how loudly she played the radio, once she was alone, there was too much silence.

They would hear from the lawyer any day. Perhaps Aunt Coco had gotten a call from Stridley that afternoon, telling her that the contracts had been signed and a settlement date set.

Would Trent come to the settlement? she wondered. No, no, of course not. He would send a representative, and that was for the best.

Besides, she had too much to do to worry about it. House hunting, the search through old papers for a clue to the emeralds' whereabouts, the classic Mustang she intended to baby along to gleaming perfection. She barely had a moment to catch her breath much less brood about seeing Trent over the settlement table.

If only it would stop hurting, even for a few moments.

It would get better, she told herself as she returned to the brake job. It had to. After they'd found a new house and settled in. After the talk of the necklace had died away. Everything would get back to normal—or what she would have to accept as normal. If the ache never completely went away, then she would learn to live with it.

She had her family. Together, they could handle anything.

Her shoulders were stiff by the time she'd finished. Rolling them a little, she started to step out from under the car when she realized the radio had stopped playing. She glanced over. And saw Trent standing by the workbench. The wrench she was holding clattered to the floor.

"What are you doing here?"

"Waiting for you to finish." She looked fabulous, was all he could think. Absolutely fabulous. "How are you?"

"Busy." Rocked from the pain, she turned to hit a button on the wall. The lift groaned as it brought the car down. "You're here about the house, I guess."

"Yes, you could say that's a large part of it."

"We've been expecting to hear from the lawyer."

"I know."

When the car was settled, she took a rag and wiped her hands, keeping her eyes on them. "Amanda's handling the details. She's at the BayWatch if you need to discuss anything."

"What I need to discuss concerns you. Us."

She looked up, then took a quick step back when she realized he'd moved over to stand next to her. "I really don't have anything else to say to you."

"Okay, then I'll do the talking. In just a minute."

He moved fast. Still, she was certain if she'd been expecting it, she could have evaded him. She wasn't certain she would have tried.

It felt so good, so right, to have his mouth covering hers, his hands framing her face. Her pride faltered long enough to have her reaching up to grasp his wrists, holding on as she let her needs flow into the kiss.

"I've thought about doing that for three and a half weeks," he murmured.

She squeezed her eyes tight. "Go away, Trent."

"Catherine—"

"Damn you, I said go away." She yanked free, then turned to brace her palms on the bench. "I hate you for coming here, for making a fool out of me again."

"You're not the fool. You never were."

When his hand brushed lightly over her shoulder, she snatched up a hammer and whirled. "If you touch me again, so help me, I'll break your nose."

He looked at her. The fire was in her eyes again. "Thank God. You're back." Delighted but cautious, he held up a hand. "Just listen, please. Business first."

"My business with you is settled."

"There's been a change in the plans." He plucked some change out of the can on the bench. "Can I buy you a drink?"

"No. Say what you have to say, then get out."

With a shrug, he strolled over to the soft drink machine and plugged in the change. It was then that C.C. noticed he was wearing scuffed high-tops.

"What are those?" she asked, staring at them.

"These?" Trent grinned as he popped the top on the can. "New shoes. What do you think?" When she simply gaped, he took a long drink. "I know, not quite the usual image, but things change. A number of things have changed. Would you mind putting down that hammer?"

"What? Oh. All right." She set it aside. "You said plans had changed. Does that mean you've decided not to buy The Towers?"

"Yes and no. Would you rather go into the office to discuss this?"

"Damn it, Trent, just tell me what's going on."

"All right. Here's the deal. We take one wing, the west, I think, so it doesn't involve Bianca's tower. We have it extensively remodeled. My preference is to salvage as much of the original material as possible and reconstruct, whenever possible, according with the original blueprints. It should maintain its turn-of-the-century feel. That will be part of the draw."

"The draw?" she repeated, lost.

"We can easily have ten suites without compromising the architecture. If memory serves, the billiard room would be excellent for dining, with the west tower remodeled for more intimate meals and private parties."

"Ten suites?"

"In the west wing," he agreed. "With an accent on aesthetics and intimacy. We'll have to put all the fire-places back in working order. I think, with what we'll offer, we'll have year-round clientele rather than just seasonal."

"What are you going to do with the rest of the house?"

"That would be up to you, and your family." He set the drink aside and came toward her. "The way I see it, you could live very easily on the first two floors and the east wing. God knows there's plenty of room."

Confused, she pressed her fingers to her temple. "We'd be, what—renting it from you?"

"That's not exactly what I had in mind. I was thinking more of a partnership." He took her hand, examining it closely. "Your knuckles have healed."

"What kind of partnership?"

"The St. James Corporation fronts the money for the renovations, advertising and so forth. Once the retreat—I like retreat better than hotel in this case— once it's in operation, we split the profits, fifty-fifty."

"I don't understand."

"It's really very simple, C.C." He lifted her hand, kissed one finger. "We compromise. We have our ho-tel, you have your home. Nobody loses."

Afraid to feel it, she banked down the little flicker of hope. "I don't see how it could work. Why would anyone want to pay to stay in someone else's home?"

"A landmark," he reminded her, and kissed an-other finger. "With a legend, a ghost and a mystery.

They'll pay very well to stay here. And when they get a taste of Coco's bouillabaisse—"

"Aunt Coco?"

"I've already offered her the position of chef. She's delighted. There's still the matter of a manager, but I think Amanda will fit the slot, don't you?" His eyes smiled as he brushed a kiss over her third finger.

"Why are you doing this?"

"I'm a businessman. It makes good business sense. I've already begun the market research." He turned her hand over and pressed his lips to the palm. "That's what I've told my board of directors. I think you know differently."

"I don't know anything." She pulled her hand away to walk to the open garage doors. "All I know is that you come back here with some sort of wild scheme—"

"It's a very solid plan," he corrected. "I'm not a wild-scheme sort of person. At least I never have been." He went to her again, taking her shoulders. "I want you to keep your home, C.C."

With her lips pressed tight, she closed her eyes. "So, you're doing it for me."

"For you, your sisters, Coco, even Bianca." Hands firm, he turned her to face him. "And I'm doing it for me. You wanted to keep me up at night, and you did."

She managed a weak smile. "Guilt works miracles."

"It has nothing to do with guilt. It never did. It has to do with love. With being in love. Don't pull away," he said quietly when she jerked against his hold.

"Business is closed for the day. Now it's just you and me. This is as personal as it gets."

At her sides, her hands clenched into fists. "It's all personal with me, don't you understand? You came here and changed everything in my life, then waltzed away again. Now you come back and tell me you've altered the plans."

"You weren't the only one things changed for. Nothing's been the same for me since I met you." Panic snaked through him. She wasn't going to give him another chance. "I didn't ask for this. I didn't want it."

"Oh, you made it abundantly clear what you didn't want." She shoved against him and got nowhere. "You have no right to start this up again."

"The hell with rights." He gave her a hard shake. "I'm trying to tell you that I love you. That's a first for me, and you're not going to turn it into an argument."

"I'll turn it into whatever I want," she tossed back, furious when her voice broke. "I'm not going to let you hurt me again. I'm not going to—" Then she went still, eyes widening. "Did you say you were in love with me?"

"Just shut up and listen. I've spent three and a half weeks feeling empty and miserable without you. I went away because I thought I could. Because I thought that was right and fair and best for both of us. Logically, it was. It still is. We're nothing alike. I couldn't see any percentage in risking both our futures when you'd certainly be better off with someone else. Someone like Finney."

"Finney?" A shout of laughter escaped. "Oh, that's rich." While her emotions whirled, she knocked a fist against his chest. "Tell you what, why don't you take your percentages back to Boston and draw a graph? Now leave me alone. I've got work to do."

"I'm not finished." When she opened her mouth to swear at him, he let instinct rule and kissed her until she quieted. As breathless as she, he rested his brow against hers. "That has nothing to do with logic or percentages." Still holding on, he took a step back so that he could see her. "Catherine, every time I reminded myself that I didn't believe in love or marriage or lifetimes, I remembered the way I felt with you."

"How? How did you feel with me?"

"Alive. Happy. And I knew I was never going to feel that way again unless I came back." He let his hands slide away. "C.C., you told me once that what we had could be the best part of my life. You were right. I don't know if I can make it work, but I need to try. I need you."

He was afraid, she realized. Even more afraid than she was. With her eyes on his, she lifted a hand to his cheek. "I can give you a guarantee on a muffler, Trent. Not on this."

"I'd settle for you telling me you still love me, that you'll give me another chance."

"I still love you. But I can't give you another chance."

"Catherine—"

"Because you haven't taken the first one yet." She touched her lips to his once, then twice. "Why don't we take it together?" she asked, then laughed when he dragged her close. "Now you've done it. You'll have grease all over you."

"I'll have to get used to it." After one last spin, he drew away to study her face. Everything he needed was right there, in her eyes. "I love you, Catherine. Very much."

She brought his hand to her cheek. "I'll have to get used to it. Maybe if you said it a few hundred times."

He told her as he held her, as he traced kisses over her face, as he lingered over the taste of her mouth.

"I think it's working," she murmured. "Maybe we should close the garage doors."

"Leave them up." He stepped back again, struggling to clear his head. "I'm still St. James enough to want to do things in their proper order, but I'm running low on control."

"What order is that?" Smiling, she ran a finger up his shirt to toy with the top button.

"Wait." Churning, he put a hand over hers. "I thought about this all the way up from Boston. It played a lot of different ways—I'd take you out again. A little wine, a lot of candlelight. Or we'd walk in the garden again at dusk."

He glanced around the garage. Honeysuckle and motor oil, he thought. Perfect.

"But this seems like the right time, the right place." He reached in his pocket for a small box, then opening it, handed it to her. "You once said if I offered you a diamond, you'd laugh in my face. I thought I might have more luck with an emerald."

Tears backed up in her throat as she stared down at the deep green stone in its simple gold setting. It gleamed up at her, full of hope and promise. "If this is a proposal, you don't need any luck at all." Wet and brilliant, her eyes came back to his. "The answer was always yes."

He slid the ring onto her finger. "Let's go home."

"Yes." Her hand linked with his. "Let's go home."

* * * * *

A Lasting Love

The passionate Cancer man is destined for love this July in Val Whisenand's FOR ETERNITY, the latest in our compelling WRITTEN IN THE STARS series.

Sexy Adam Gaines couldn't explain the eerie sense of familiarity that arose each time his eyes met Kate Faraday's. But Mexico's steamy jungles were giving the star-crossed lovers another chance to make their love last for all eternity....

FOR ETERNITY by Val Whisenand is coming this July from Silhouette Romance. It's WRITTEN IN THE STARS!

JULYSTAR

Take 4 bestselling love stories FREE

Plus get a FREE surprise gift!

Special Limited-time Offer

Mail to
Silhouette Reader Service™
P.O. Box 609
Fort Erie, Ontario
L2A 5X3

YES! Please send me 4 free Silhouette Romance™ novels and my free surprise gift. Then send me 6 brand-new novels every month, which I will receive months before they appear in bookstores. Bill me at the low price of $2.25 each—a saving of 25¢ apiece off cover prices plus only 69¢ per shipment for delivery. I understand that accepting the books and gift places me under no obligation ever to buy any books. I can always return a shipment and cancel at any time. Even if I never buy another book from Silhouette, the 4 free books and the surprise gift are mine to keep forever.

315 BPA AC7M

Name	(PLEASE PRINT)	
Address		Apt. No.
City	Prov.	Postal Code

This offer is limited to one order per household and not valid to present Silhouette Romance™ subscribers. Terms and prices are subject to change. Canadian residents add applicable federal and provincial taxes.

SROM-BPACDADR

© 1990 Harlequin Enterprises Limited

THE
CALHOUN WOMEN

BY NORA ROBERTS

If you've enjoyed COURTING CATHERINE in the Silhouette
Romance line, be sure to look for the rest of THE CALHOUN
WOMEN titles in other Silhouette series over the next
three months.

July
A MAN FOR AMANDA
Silhouette Desire #649

August
FOR THE LOVE OF LILAH
Silhouette Special Edition #685

September
SUZANNA'S SURRENDER
Silhouette Intimate Moments #397

Silhouette Romance—Love, at its most tender, provocative,
emotional... in stories that will make you laugh and cry
while bringing you the magic of falling in love.

To try other Silhouette Romance titles, please see special
savings offer on the back.

CWSR

 *Silhouette Books*®

Silhouette Romance®